# JOSHUA AND THE MAGICAL ISLANDS

## PORTALLAS BOOK 2

By Christopher D. Morgan

This novel has been written using British English spelling and conventions.

*Joshua and the Magical Islands* is book 2 in the Portallas series.

Second edition (published November 2017)

Edited by Gordon Long
Cover design by Christian Bentulan

50,915 words.

ISBN-13 (hardback): 978-0-9945257-8-9
ISBN-13 (paperback): 978-0-9945257-7-2
ISBN-13 (e-book): 978-0-9945257-6-5

www.dragonrealmpress.com

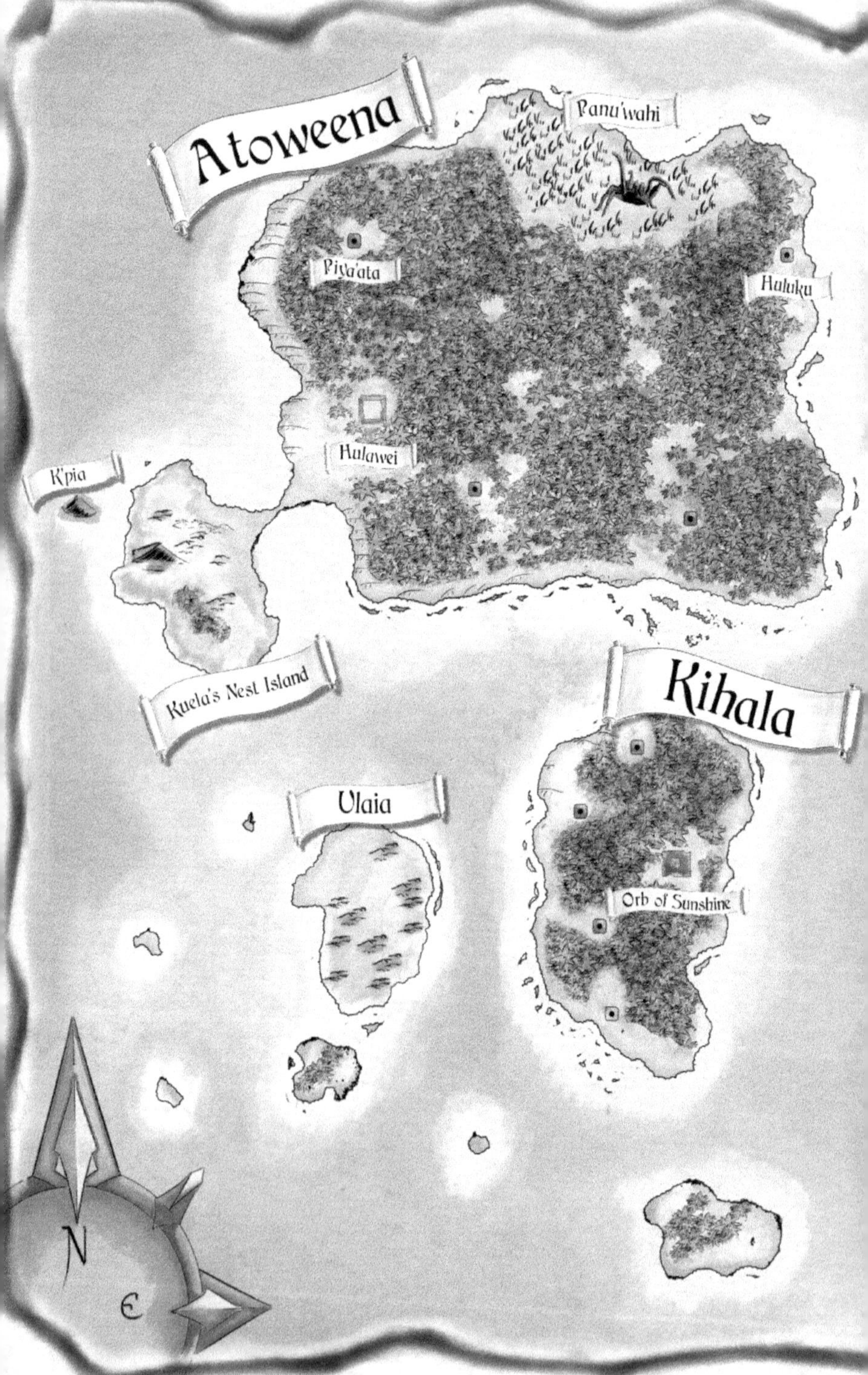

Atoweena
Panu'wahi
Piya'ata
Haluku
Hulawei
K'pia
Kuela's Nest Island
Kihala
Ulaia
Orb of Sunshine
N
E

Lua'pele
ARCHIPELAGO
Joshua and the Magical Islands

# CHAPTER ONE
## *Morelle*

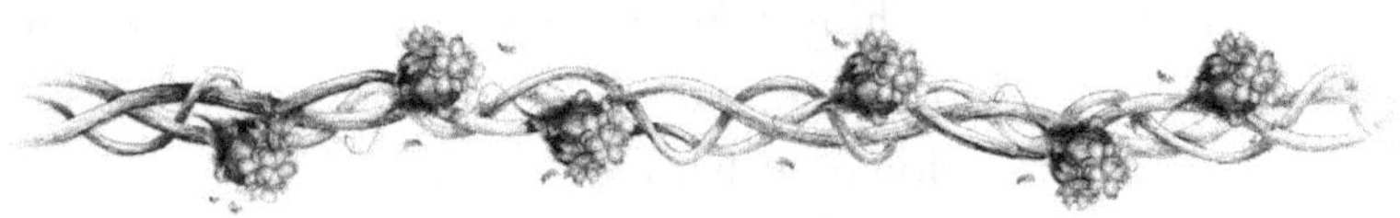

Joshua and Sarah strolled happily through the forest towards Morelle. With the turmoil of the battle against the Goat and His Blood-bats at Jemarrah behind them, and nobody chasing after them anymore, they felt much more relaxed as they walked hand in hand.

Now that he and his girlfriend were less than a day's travel from his home village, Joshua was both excited and nervous about introducing Sarah to his mother.

Sarah gazed into Joshua's eyes and smiled.

"You know you have mud down the side of your nose," she laughed at him.

Joshua laughed back. He reached into his keeper bag and took out a small, oval mirror with a short, wooden handle. It was the Mirror of Prophecy he had been given by Fable back at Fable and Florelle's Inn. He stared at it to see what Sarah was talking about. He stopped walking and froze, staring into the mirror, his mouth open and his eyes wide.

Sarah's smile faded. "Joshua? What is it?"

He turned and gazed at her. More than anything else, he loved Sarah's deep, blue eyes. He'd do almost anything to catch a moment admiring them. But this time it was different. This time, Joshua feared for Sarah.

She sensed something was wrong and asked softly, "Joshua, what is it?"

A look of terror formed on his face. "The Goat. He's still alive!"

Sarah stared back at him in horror. He turned and set off at a brisk pace through the forest with Sarah chasing after him. "Joshua, wait! Slow down! What did you see?"

"Come on!" he said, beckoning her to hurry.

They soon reached the outer boundary of Morelle, where they had planned to meet Andrew, who had travelled back with Galleon a few days earlier.

"That's strange," Joshua said, looking around.

"What's the matter?"

"He's not here. He was supposed to meet us here, right? That is what he said, right?"

"Maybe he just forgot."

"Andrew? That's not like him. No, something is wrong. I can feel it."

"Oh, come on, Joshua, don't you think you're jumping to conclusions? There could be a dozen reasons why he's not here."

Joshua fixed his eyes on the ground, shaking his head.

"No. Something's definitely wrong."

He turned towards Morelle, and they hurried off again.

As they neared the village, they both sensed something was amiss and approached with caution. An eerie mist hung in the air as they crept into Morelle. There were no people coming or going. The forest was deathly quiet.

"Can you smell that?" Sarah asked. "Like…smoke."

Joshua nodded. A light breeze started to clear the hazy mist. As it did, Joshua froze at what he saw. Chills ran down his spine. The hair on the back of his neck stood up, and his heart skipped a beat.

A scene of total devastation appeared through the acrid smoke. All the buildings in Morelle had been burned. Joshua's home village was reduced to ashes.

The roofs were all gone, and the few remaining beams were smouldering. Plumes of smoke drifted into the air. Sarah gasped, raising her hand to her mouth.

They pushed on through the burned remains, trying to see if they could find anyone. The entire village was deathly quiet with not a soul in sight.

Joshua stopped in front of what was left of the Elder's hut. Atop the remnants of its roof stood a post with a black flag flapping in the wind. Across the face of the flag was the unmistakable mark of The Goat.

"Where is everybody?" Sarah asked in shock as she surveyed the devastation before them. The scene was uncomfortably familiar to that of the Valley of Moross they had encountered when they were looking for the Oracle of Forestium a few days ago. All the people of the valley had been banished to another world by the Goat and the only things left were the burned-out shells of huts.

"He has them," Joshua said quietly.

Sarah looked at him with grave concern. "What was it, Joshua? What did you see in the Mirror of Prophecy back there?"

Joshua turned and put his hand on Sarah's shoulder. "Death," he replied after a long pause. "I saw someone die in my arms."

Sarah looked stunned. "Who was it?" she asked with bated breath.

Joshua surveyed the sight of destruction around him. He shook his head slowly. "I don't know who it was. The image was hazy, and I didn't see her face clearly."

Joshua struggled to figure out who the figure in the mirror could have been. "It was…a girl…I think. She had two colourful feathers in her hair. But I couldn't quite…I…I just don't know."

"What happened to everyone here?" Sarah asked.

The present situation now started to sink in with Joshua. Morelle wasn't just a village. He recalled a lifetime of experiences. When he saw his home, he didn't see a familiar wooden hut made from logs and moss, he saw memories of a happy childhood. Everything that Joshua was—everything that made him the person he was; all his triumphs and failures, all his hopes and dreams—was now reduced to ashes. Joshua shook his head, a tear welling in his eye. He wrapped his arms around Sarah and broke down. The two comforted each other in their moment of despair.

Finally, Joshua and Sarah turned and continued through the ruins of Morelle, looking for survivors. It was the same at every building; everything was burned, but there was no sign of any bodies. It was as if everyone had just vanished and the village had then been destroyed.

Joshua stopped in front of his mother's hut. The roof was missing, and most of the walls were no longer standing. What was left of the furniture was now a pile of smouldering ash. A black cauldron lay smashed across the floor in what was once the kitchen. Beside it was a scorched wooden doll. Joshua picked it up.

"What's that?" Sarah asked.

Joshua caught her eye. He tried to force a smile as he brushed soot from the toy. It wasn't just a doll. The tattered figure represented much more than that. A flood of happy memories surfaced. In his mind's eye, Joshua watched wood shavings drop to the ground as his mother carved it from the Ashfer tree branch he had brought home with him one day. She had spent weeks carving, shaping, bringing the toy to life. He remembered being so pleased when it was finished, and he was allowed to play with it.

"Mum made it for me when I was small," he explained, a smile forming. "She was clutching it when I told her I was leaving Morelle."

Sarah reached over and gently put her hand on his shoulder. "How could the Goat have done this?"

"I don't know," Joshua said turning to look at her. There was despair in his tone. He pursed his lips and breathed a heavy sigh.

"He has them all," he said looking around. Anger welled inside. Joshua felt a sickening sensation in the pit of his stomach. After all he had been through, after defeating the Goat's dark forces, after losing his father, and now this? *It mustn't be in vain. I have to do something.*

"We have to find them," he proclaimed. "We have to find them and bring them back." Joshua's breathing quickened. Emotions he had ever tapped into surfaced like an erupting volcano inside him. "And when I do," he declared, "I'm going to make him pay for what he's done. I'm going to kill him."

# CHAPTER TWO
## *Orb of Sacrifice*

The distant shriek of a Raetheon pierced the sombre atmosphere. The majestic bird circled the village high above the treetop canopy. As Joshua looked up to see if he could spot it, he heard a faint voice.

"Joshua—"

Startled, he and Sarah spun around to find the source of the sound.

"Joshua," the voice called again, "help me."

The cry came from beneath a pile of scorched wood embers. Joshua and Sarah dug through the hot charcoal. They yanked at the smouldering remains, tossing them aside, trying not to burn themselves in the process.

A charred and blood-stained hand reached up from beneath the pile and Joshua grabbed it. As Sarah removed the remaining pieces of debris, Protello's face stared up at them. His breathing was laboured, and he looked at Joshua with beseeching eyes. Joshua knelt down and cradled him. The dying Metamorph could barely support the weight of his own head and struggled to lock his focus onto Joshua's face.

"Protello, what happened?" Joshua asked frantically.

"It was the Goat," Joshua's friend whispered. He gasped for each breath. "Only you can rescue them, Joshua."

He lifted his hand and opened his fingers to reveal an orb exactly like the three Joshua had used before to help him open the Portallas. Engraved on this crystal was the shape of a coffin.

"This is the Orb of Sacrifice," Protello murmured. His voice was now but a faint whisper. "My death…will activate it. You must get to the other side and…open the next Portallas. Open them all, Joshua. Only then can you hope to defeat Him. Find the others and…open…open them all—"

Protello coughed and spluttered blood, which showered Joshua's hands and arms. The sight of Protello in such pain was gut-wrenching. It scared Joshua, but he tried to remain strong for his dying friend. The Metamorph's voice softened further, and his body was now completely limp.

"Please, Joshua, you have already opened the Portallas in this world. You must…open them all…do this before…before it's too…"

Protello was unable to finish the sentence. Joshua felt the life slipping away from the Metamorph. Joshua's friend gasped his last lungful of air, and his head fell to one side.

After a few seconds, Sarah felt Protello's lifeless wrist. She glanced at Joshua and slowly shook her head. "He's gone," she said quietly.

A tear ran down Joshua's cheek. Very slowly, he put his hand to Protello's face and lowered the Metamorph's eyelids. Within seconds, Protello's limp body began to disintegrate, until it finally turned to dust, falling through Joshua's arms and into the pile of rubble beneath him.

As it did so, the orb in Joshua's hand started to vibrate and hum quietly. The humming grew louder, and the crystal began to pulsate with ever increasing flashes of light.

Joshua and Sarah stood up. As the wind carried the ashes of Protello's body into the air, there was a blinding flash of light from the orb. Joshua dropped the crystal, and a vortex opened up right above it with such intensity that it threw them both to the ground. Leaves and branches were carried into the air by the deafening wind, swirling around the vortex.

Through the torrent of air, Joshua could see a sandy beach. Clear blue waters crashed onto the sand. Thick palm trees with enormous green leaves dangling all the way to the ground lined the shore. Joshua and Sarah turned to each other with puzzled looks. It was unlike anything either of them had ever seen.

"Where is that place?" Sarah shouted above the noise of the rushing wind. Her hair blew about with such force she had to use both hands to keep it from her eyes.

"I don't know," Joshua shouted back, "but it must be where all the others are."

"We should go through, as Protello told us," Sarah shouted at the top of her voice. The vortex picked up debris and embers from all over the village and tossed them about like matchsticks in a tornado. Joshua and Sarah had to keep dodging larger flying objects. As the two of them regarded each other wondering what they should do, the vortex started to dissipate, and the image of the sandy beach began to recede.

"Quick!" Joshua screamed. "It's closing. If we don't go now, it'll be too late."

He reached for the orb, grabbed Sarah's hand and they both jumped into the vortex. The deafening rush of wind swirled around them violently. Joshua heard Sarah screaming but lost sight of her. He was disoriented and no longer sure which way was up. Everything went dark, and he felt all his senses ebb away.

# CHAPTER THREE

## *Luana*

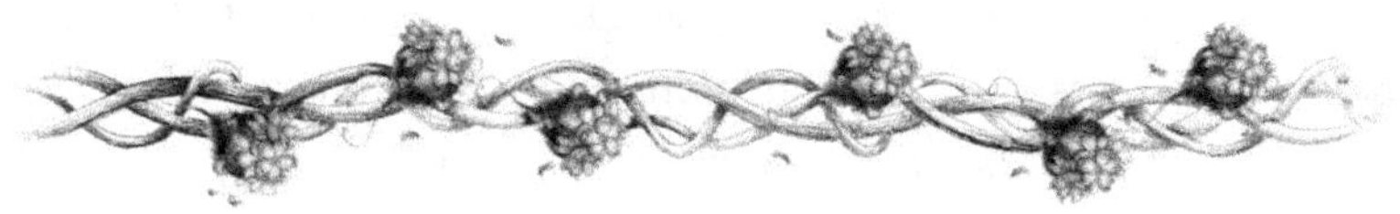

Unaware of how much time had passed, Joshua slowly became aware of his surroundings. The first of his senses to return was his hearing. A strange noise came from all around him, unlike anything he had ever heard before. The sound was comforting, like a pleasant lullaby. At first, he thought it was the cooing of a Raetheon, but it wasn't quite the same.

A warm sensation crept up his legs. It came and went repeatedly. There was a recurring sound each time he felt the warmth.

The veil of fog in his mind lifted, and he could start to see patches of light through his eyelids. As he lay there, his senses slowly returned.

He was lying on the ground. It felt soft. As he tried opening his eyes, the bright light forced them to close again. Curious as to where he was, he struggled against the glare. The blinding sun was directly overhead.

The young Woodsman raised his hand to his face to shield it from the penetrating rays until a cloudless, blue sky in all directions came into focus.

Still disoriented, he pushed himself into an upright position and peered out onto a body of water before him. He squinted, his eyes still adjusting to the unfamiliar surroundings.

Gentle waves splashed over his legs every few seconds. The water was warm and crystal clear. Still dazed and confused, he tried to figure out where he was.

He was sitting on a long stretch of white, sandy beach. It was just like the image he saw in the Orb of Sacrifice before they entered the vortex. Unfamiliar with these new sensations, he held his hands to his face, loosening dried sand, which fell to the ground.

Then he heard a moan. Sarah was off to his left, lying on her side, facing away from him. He reached over and nudged her shoulder. She roused and turned to look at him.

"Where…where are we?" She raised her hand to her face to shield her eyes from the blinding sun as her senses, too, awakened.

Joshua stood up, then helped Sarah to her feet.

"I don't know," he said, taking a good look around, "doesn't it look familiar to you? You've travelled to more places in Forestium than I have."

Everything about this place looked, felt and smelled unfamiliar to Joshua. The sun was much warmer. The familiar violet of Forestium skies was replaced by a deep blue. He had never seen such an open expanse of clear, blue water before. There was a salty taste in his mouth with every breath he took. The trees were different—much shorter than usual. Even the soft, white sand beneath his feet was foreign. He tried to take it all in.

Two islands appeared across the water. Joshua thought these at first to be a mirage, but both came into sharp focus once he was on his feet. Thick vegetation covered one and but other, much smaller, was rocky and barren.

The white, sandy beach they found themselves standing on stretched into the distance in both directions. Behind them, the sand gave way to palm trees with huge trunks. Each was topped with three or four enormous, green leaves that were so big they drooped all the way to the ground, casting dark shadows beneath them. They were unlike any tree or plant Joshua had ever seen.

"Um, something tells me we're not in Forestium anymore," Sarah said.

Joshua snapped his attention back to her.

"What do you mean we're not in Forestium anymore? Are…are you sure?"

Sarah looked in both directions. "A palm-tree-lined beach this size?"

"Let's go inland," Joshua suggested. "It'll at least give us cover from the sun."

Sarah nodded in agreement, and two of them clambered off the beach and into the shade of the thick vegetation. The relief the palm leaves offered from the blistering heat of the sun was immediate and welcome.

They hadn't gone far before Sarah held her hand out to stop Joshua. There before them stood a girl, staring at them.

She was a little shorter than Sarah with similar blond hair. Her skin was beautifully tanned all over. Tied into her hair at the top were three long, beautifully coloured feathers. There was an awkward silence as the three of them continued to stare at each other. The curious-looking girl was the first to speak.

"You're not from around here, are you?" she asked in a commanding tone. She had a soft timbre to her voice, but there was an air of confidence about her.

"Um, no, we're not," Joshua replied, returning the smile. "We're, um—"

He paused for a moment and lowered his brow as he realised he wasn't sure how to respond. He turned to Sarah.

"Well, we're…from another place," Sarah added, nodding at Joshua. "I'm Sarah, and this is Joshua."

The girl walked up to the two outsiders and peered at them inquisitively. As she walked around them studying them carefully, feeling their clothes and hair, Joshua regarded her as well.

She was wearing a skirt made from dried reeds and a green top fashioned from pieces of leaves from one of the palm trees. She wore nothing on her feet and carried no weapons, as far as he could tell. She completed a full circle of the two strangers before stopping in front of them.

"I'm Luana," she finally said. "Welcome to Atoweena. Where have you come from? Have you been here long? How did you get here? We don't get many outsiders. Have you travelled far?"

"Um, Atoweena, did you say?" Joshua asked. Somewhat bewildered by all the questions, he wanted to redirect the attention away from them.

"That's right," Luana said with a nod, "it's one of the islands of Archipelago."

"Archipelago?" Sarah asked, looking confused. "Is that the name of this place?"

The young woman nodded again. She eyed them both up and down.

"You're really not from this world, are you?"

Joshua and Sarah turned each other.

"We're…we're from another world," Joshua finally said. "A place we call…Forestium."

Luana eyed them both suspiciously.

"Well, how did you get here, then? Did you come the same way the other one did?"

Joshua's eyes widened.

"Other one? You mean there are others like us here?"

"Mmm. He looks just like you," she said pointing at Joshua.

"W-where is he? Is he okay? Has he been here long? C-can you take us to him?" Sarah asked, eagerly.

She and Joshua stared at the young woman with bated breath.

"Well…if I take you to him," she said tentatively, "will you tell me more about this Forestium place you come from? I'm an explorer. I want to know all there is to know about your world."

Joshua and Sarah looked at each other and smiled.

"Of course," Sarah said, beaming with excitement. "We're kind of explorers too. Well, we're not really explorers. I'm a Fixer actually. I guess we are explorers a little. I mean, we're here in your world, right? I guess that makes us explorers."

Joshua cleared his throat and nudged Sarah.

"Oh, yes. Well, I'll tell you all about Forestium, but we must first find our people. Can you help us?"

Luana tilted her head as if to ponder the question. "Come on," she said, "I'll take you back to my village. The Protector is with him."

The three of them set off farther inland and away from the beach.

"How many strangers from our world have come here?" Joshua asked.

"I don't know exactly," Luana replied. She was studying his keeper bag, and the slingshot hooked onto his weapon belt. "There's just the one on Atoweena so far as I know," she said pulling on the slingshot elastic, "but there may be other strangers on some of the other islands too. What are these things?"

Joshua unclipped his slingshot and showed it to her.

"Oh, um, this is a slingshot. I use it for, um, hunting."

Luana regarded him, puzzled. "You catch fish with this?" she asked, lowering her brow and handing it back to him.

"Well, maybe not fish. Here, let me show you."

They stopped walking, and Joshua searched until he found a pebble, which he loaded into the pouch of his slingshot. Pulling back on the elastic vine, he launched it into the treetop canopy. It shot up and struck one of the huge palm leaves. Instead of penetrating the foliage, as Joshua thought it might, it rebounded and fell to the ground. Several birds took to the air, startled, and disappeared through the thick layers of green palm leaves. Luana's eyes gleamed, and her jaw dropped.

"Wow! Can you show me how to make one of these things?"

"Sure," Joshua replied, "but first we need to see this other stranger you mentioned."

"Come," she started walking again. "It's not far from here."

The palm trees soon gave way to a clearing. Within it were a dozen or more structures with thatched roofs. They were about the same size as the huts from Joshua's village but were unlike anything he'd seen before.

Each was round and made from dozens of tightly packed, vertical, wooden branches. The branches were tied together with the same dried reeds from which the thatched roofs were made.

As in Forestium, they appeared to be made from the materials that grew all around them.

"These people have much in common with us, I think," Joshua said to Sarah, who nodded. She was staring at everything gleefully, like she had entered a new world of discovery.

The buildings were arranged in a circle around the edge of the clearing with a larger, similar structure in the centre. Twenty or so people milled around the small village. All of them stopped what they were doing and stared at Joshua and Sarah as Luana led them to the central building.

The people had dark skin, like Luana, and wore simple clothing made from reeds and other natural materials. The men—all muscular and tall—had tattoos on their bodies and feathers dangling from string tied around their arms and legs. The women wore tops decorated with the same colourful feathers that Luana had in her hair. Two men stood by a fire pit in the centre of the clearing, prodding it with spears. A half-cooked animal was suspended above the fire. One of the women was rotating it slowly as it cooked.

"This is Hulawei, where I live." She indicated the central structure. "Come, the other stranger is inside."

Like the smaller buildings, this much larger one was round. It had a cone-shaped roof with walls made from vertical lengths of tree branches. All the villagers' eyes continued to follow the three of them as they entered.

Joshua and Sarah followed Luana inside. A small fire burned in the centre, encircled by stones. White smoke drifted up to the ceiling and went out through a hole at the very top. The smell that hung in the air reminded Joshua of the burned-out shells of huts in Forestium. It was a stark reminder of what had recently happened back in Morelle.

As they walked around to the far side of the fire, Joshua saw two people sitting on a pile of leaves on the floor. He recognised the unmistakable outline of one of them.

# CHAPTER FOUR

## *The Protector of Atoweena*

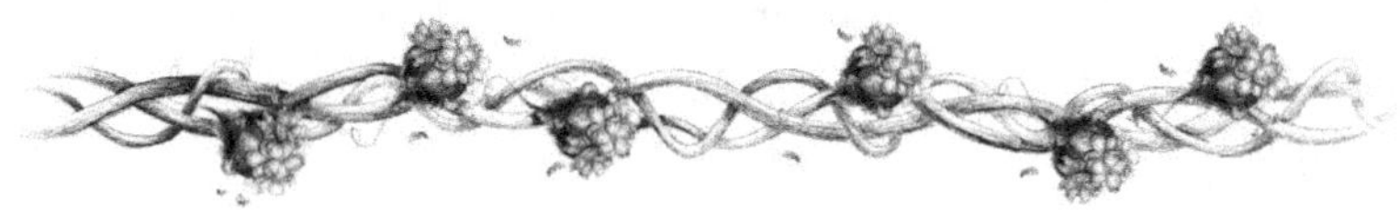

"Andrew?" Joshua called out.

Andrew turned his head and beamed with delight. He jumped up to greet them. "Joshua! Sarah? What? How? I mean, where did you come from? How did you get here?"

"We came to rescue you, of course," Sarah grinned.

"How did you get here?" Joshua asked.

"I don't know," Andrew said, shaking his head. "Galleon and I were on the outskirts of Morelle, waiting for the two of you to arrive. The next thing I know, I was on the ground looking up at a couple of strangers. They brought me to this village and I've been here ever since. I don't even know where this place is. They haven't really told me anything. Where are we? We're definitely not in Morelle anymore."

"We're not even in Forestium anymore," Joshua replied, shaking his head. "This is a different world. Our new friend here called it Archipelago. How long ago did you arrive?"

"I'm not sure. Not long I think; it's hard to tell. I've no idea how long I was unconscious on the ground before they found me. I don't know what happened to Galleon either."

"Have you seen anyone else from Morelle?" Sarah asked.

"No. Why?" Andrew clearly thought it an odd question. "What's happened? What is this place and why are we here?"

The man who had been sitting with Andrew spoke for the first time. He was an imposing figure, with tattoos up and down his arms and shoulders. At full height, he was easily the tallest of them all, with a very stocky build. Like Luana, he had tanned skin and was wearing simple clothing made from reeds and leaves.

"Your friend called you Joshua," he said to Joshua, "and Sarah?"

He spoke with a deep and commanding voice. Joshua nodded.

"Welcome to Hulawei. My name is Paleki. I am Protector of Atoweena Island."

He raised his fist to his chest and bowed his head slightly.

"We found your friend here not long ago outside the village. He's very lucky to be alive. Had we not found him when we did, he would have been eaten by Palm Crabs. I thought it best to have him brought to the village until we could learn more about where he came from and what he is doing here."

Joshua and Sarah both looked at Andrew with confused looks on their faces.

"Palm Crabs?" Sarah asked, raising her brow.

"Vicious creatures," Luana said. "They invade the islands from time to time. They are —"

Luana's explanation was cut short by a strange noise outside that drew everyone's attention. It was the same pleasant sound Joshua remembered hearing when he woke up on the beach.

"What's that sound?" Joshua asked.

"A message," Paleki said, looking at the door.

As he spoke, a beautiful, brightly coloured bird flew gracefully in, then circled twice above their heads.

It was bright red and green, about half the size of a full-grown Raetheon. It had beautiful plumage with four silvery-blue tail feathers like those Luana had tied into her hair. The graceful bird had a beautiful, bright yellow bill as long as a forearm.

Paleki held out his wrist and the magnificent creature glided over and landed gently on it. It folded its wings, singing softly. A small tube was attached to its leg. Paleki pulled out a piece of parchment from the tube.

The bird stretched its wings and took off again. It circled a few times before gliding effortlessly out through the door again and was off.

"That's beautiful," Sarah said. "What was it?"

"It's a Kuela," Luana replied. "They deliver messages between villages on different islands. They can also read our thoughts."

Frowning, Paleki took his time reading the parchment.

"It is from the Protector of Kihala. Another stranger has been found there," he finally said, continuing to regard the parchment with a puzzled look on his face.

"What is it?" Luana asked, looking concerned. Paleki's eyes shifted between them.

"It is a…half man," he said slowly, squinting at the parchment.

"Galleon!" Joshua, Sarah and Andrew all said in unison.

"He's a friend of ours," Andrew said smiling at Paleki.

"Hmm. Andrew, here said he doesn't know how he arrived," Paleki said turning to Joshua again.

"Well, we think he was brought here, along with many others from my village, against his will," Joshua said.

"And you were brought here against your will too?"

"Um…well, actually, no. We sort of came here by choice."

Paleki peered at him intently. "Really? What sort of magic can bring someone here from another world?" he asked, folding his arms.

Andrew, too, looked at Joshua expectantly.

Joshua turned to Sarah for support but she just shrugged. He reached into his keeper bag and took out the Orb of Sacrifice Protello had given him and showed it to Paleki.

Both Paleki and Luana took one look at it and dropped to their knees with their heads bowed.

"The Orb of Sunshine," Paleki said in a quiet, reverent tone.

He then spoke an incantation in a strange language. Once finished, he hesitantly peered at the crystal.

"How is it that you have the Orb of Sunshine?"

"No, you don't understand," Joshua said. "This is the Orb of Sacrifice. It's what we used to get here."

Paleki squinted at Joshua and gingerly reached out to take the Orb. He inspected the engraving of the coffin on the side and then slowly stood up.

"I see," he said, studying the crystal carefully. "There is another orb here in Archipelago. It is very much like this one, except…the carving here…it is different."

Paleki pointed to the carving on the side of the crystal in the shape of a coffin. "We call ours the Orb of Sunshine: a sacred thing to us. It is said to have magical powers."

"Really? Where is it?" Joshua asked with wide eyes.

Luana reached over to take a closer look at the orb. "Kihala," she said, gingerly rubbing her finger over the orb in awe. "It's the same island where this half-man friend of yours was found. I can take you if you want."

Joshua and Sarah both beamed at her, nodding excitedly.

"Yes please," Joshua said. Paleki handed the Orb of Sacrifice back and Joshua slipped it back into his keeper bag.

"Come," Luana said. "If we go now, we can make Kihala before nightfall."

They bid farewell to the Protector, and Luana led them out of the hut.

Christopher D. Morgan

# CHAPTER FIVE

## *The Makeshift Boat*

Luana led them out of the village towards the setting sun.

"Where did you get the Orb of Sacrifice from?" Andrew asked Joshua.

"Protello gave it to us," Sarah said, mournfully. "We found him when we got back to Morelle."

"Protello? How is he?" Andrew asked.

Joshua's heart sank as he remembered his last encounter with the Metamorph.

"I'm afraid he's dead," Joshua answered. "Giving me the orb was the last thing he did before he —"

Andrew stopped in his tracks. "Dead? W…what do you mean? What happened?"

"I'm not sure," Joshua searched for the right words, "when we got back to Morelle, everyone had disappeared and everything was burned to the ground. It was just like the Valley of Moross. We found Protello under a pile of burned remains. I don't know where everyone went but I'm hoping they're all safe and somewhere here in Archipelago. You're the first person we've found from Morelle so far. Can you remember anything about what happened?"

Andrew's let out a deep sigh, shaking his head. He looked at Joshua and Sarah in turn, struggling to come to grips with it all.

"It…it was like I said. One minute everything was fine, and the next I woke up here. I…I don't remember anything about Morelle burning or people being taken away or anything like that. Why would anyone want to take people from Morelle and burn it to the ground? I can't believe it."

"I think it was the Goat," Joshua said.

Andrew's shoulders sank. He titled his head and said, "But…I thought…I thought we killed him. How can he still be alive?"

"The Goat?" Luana asked curiously.

Joshua realised that none of this would make sense to her. "He's an all-powerful, magical being we encountered back at home. He has banished people from our world in the past. We think he might be responsible this time, as well."

"Luana, have your people encountered the Goat before? Have you heard of him at all?" Sarah asked.

Luana thought for a moment. "Well, I've explored many of the islands of Archipelago, perhaps more than anyone else, but there are hundreds more that even I haven't visited yet. If this Goat of yours exists, I've never seen or heard of him. The only things we have to worry about are Palm Crabs. I hate those creatures."

"You'd be scared of the Goat if you ever encountered him," Andrew said. "Crabs would be the least of your worries. What's so dangerous about crabs anyway? Surely you can just walk out of their way or kick them or something?"

"Didn't you see the Palm Crabs that nearly got to you when you arrived?" Luana snapped at him.

"Well…no," Andrew said, looking a little sheepish.

"So, you've never actually seen one then, right?"

"Well, no, but a crab's a crab, right?" Andrew gave a nervous chuckle.

Luana glared at him. The grin on his face slowly disappeared.

"They are about as big as you are. Their pincers can cut clean through bone. Two of them would easily be strong enough to pull you into the ocean. Almost nothing can kill them. Only the sharpest of spears can penetrate their shells."

Andrew's face turned pale.

"My baby sister, Kalena, was taken by those vile creatures in the night," Luana recalled with a sombre look on her face. "The whole village went out looking for her the next morning but the only thing we found was a sandal on the beach. Palm Crab tracks were everywhere."

Sarah's hand shot to her mouth as she took a sharp intake of breath.

"Luana, that's…just awful."

Luana lowered her head. "Look," she said, "just don't get too complacent. Be on your guard—especially after dark. If you hear clicking sounds in the night, look for their brightly lit eyes."

"And exactly what do we do if we see them?" Andrew asked.

Luana glared at Andrew. After a long pause, she sighed. "Run. Their shell is so tough, you can't pierce it unless you have a spear and a very strong arm. If they grab you, their claws have razor-sharp edges that can rip right through limbs. The only real defence is to not be there. Hardly anyone survives an attack from those fouls beasts."

She walked on. The others pondered her words as they followed her.

They eventually made their way to a beach on the south side of the island, from which they could see even more islands across the water.

Luana pointed to one in particular. "That's Kihala. That's where the Orb of Sunshine is."

Joshua looked up and down the white sandy beach. It was featureless. Nothing resembling a boat or raft was anywhere in sight.

"So, how do we get there? It looks too far to swim."

"By palm frond, of course," Luana replied casually.

She walked over to the line of palm trees with their enormous, solid green leaves and grabbed the end of one that drooped low enough that she could reach its tip. She pulled on it hard. It came away from the tree, and she dragged it onto the beach. Strands of thin fibres extended from the sides of the huge leaf along both edges. Luana knelt down at one end of the leaf and bent its edges towards each other, tying the ends of the strands together. As she did this, the enormous frond started to take the shape of a boat. She finished with a boat-shaped leaf that would easily fit them all in. Luana dragged the vessel into the water.

"That's ingenious," Sarah said exclaimed, "but what are we going to use to paddle through the water?"

Luana smiled. She walked back to the row of palm trees again and rummaged on the ground, where some large nuts lay at the base of the palm's trunk. She picked up a few and brought them back to the makeshift boat.

"I'm not getting in that," Andrew objected. "W…what if it sinks?"

Luana just smiled. "Where's your sense of adventure?" She finished loading the nuts into the boat and motioned for everyone to get in.

"Don't worry," Joshua said to Andrew with a chuckle, "I'm sure it'll be fine if Luana says so."

He leaned towards Luana and whispered in her ear. "It *will* be fine, won't it?"

"Here," Luana said to Sarah, winking at Joshua. She handed Sarah one of the nuts. "Open these by pulling on the husks."

Sarah pulled the husk from either side of the nut and pried it into two halves. Inside each half were hundreds of tiny seedpods.

"Wow! Look at these," Sarah said, giddy with excitement "what do I do with them?"

"Hold on and don't drop them," Luana motioned everyone to follow her as she pulled the boat out onto the water. "We need to get out of the shallows first."

They were about knee deep when Luana beckoned them to get into the makeshift boat. She pulled it farther out into the shallows for some distance. When it got so deep that her chest was just above the water, she deftly climbed in. Sarah sat at the back of the boat with the open nuts.

"Right, Sarah," Luana said, "start throwing some of those seeds behind you, but only a few at a time. Keep throwing them every few seconds."

Sarah did as she was told. As the small seedpods hit the water, the outer shells dissolved, releasing thousands of tiny seedlings, which glisten with tiny flashes of light, like stars. It made the water look like the night sky, with a myriad of shining specks of light. Fish swam up to feed on the twinkling seeds. It was just a few at first but soon there were hundreds and then thousands of the fish all racing up towards the flashing seeds. Before long, the water darkened and ripples formed on the surface.

"Whoa…w-what's h-happening?" Andrew stuttered with a hint of panic in his voice as the boat bobbed up and down with the increasing ripples.

Luana smiled. "Wait and see."

After a few seconds, the ripples intensified, lifting the rear end of the makeshift boat up and down. The ripples soon turned into waves.

Luana reached out over the front end of the boat and leaned in the direction of Kihala Island. Sarah continued sprinkling the seeds into the water behind them. The waves increased so much that the boat started surfing the leading edge. The craft soon matched the speed of the intense surf and was propelled forward.

Luana steered the boat by shifting her weight. Patches of darkened water created by the feeding frenzy of fish followed behind them. Whatever they were, the sheer numbers of them generated a continuous wave that pushed the frond across the water.

Splashes of salty water mixed with the rush of fast moving air as the boat raced across the stretch of water between the islands. Everyone was getting wet from the spray. The salty taste was foreign to the visiting forest-dwellers but the sensation was exhilarating at the same time. The sea breeze rushed so fast and loud, nobody was able to speak but everyone had huge smiles on their faces. The water splashing on their faces and lips had a fishy taste to it. Joshua and Sarah were enjoying these new sensations. Andrew's face was turning pale.

After a few minutes of racing towards the other shore, the colour of the water lightened as the boat entered the shallows around Kihala. Sarah stopped feeding seeds to the fish and the wave slowly dissipated. The boat's own momentum carried them the rest of the way, and they drifted to the beach.

The makeshift boat hit the shore and ground to a halt, and everyone lurched forward. Luana jumped out and grabbed the front end. They all got out and stepped onto the beach.

"Wasn't that the most incredible thing?" Joshua exclaimed.

"That was absolutely amazing!" Sarah agreed.

"I think I'm going to vomit," Andrew said, his face a distinct shade of green.

Joshua helped Luana pull their ingenious transport out of the water and up onto the sloping sand.

"What was causing those waves?" he asked.

"We call them Dauphins."

"What do they look like?" Sarah asked.

"I don't know," Luana shrugged, "I've never actually seen one out of the water. Shall we go?"

Christopher D. Morgan

# CHAPTER SIX
## *Kihala*

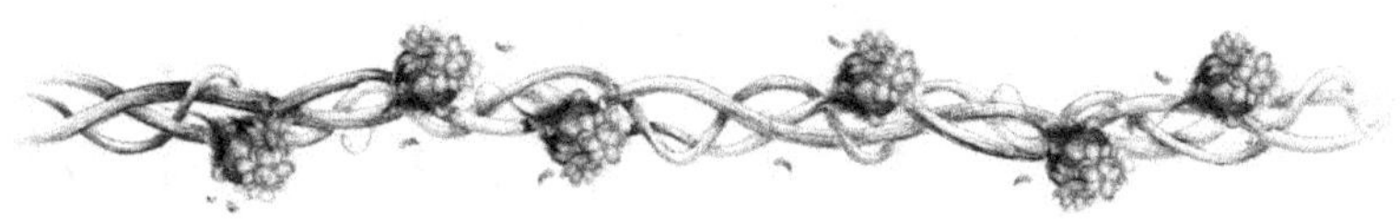

Kihala seemed very much like Atoweena, the island they had just come from. It had the same white sand and was overgrown with the same thick palm trees with wide leaves stretching outwards and drooping towards the ground.

"So, where do we go to find our friend, Galleon?" Joshua asked Luana.

"We'll have to go and see the Protector of this island first."

"Is that the custom here, Luana? Do you have to see the Protector each time you visit one of the island?"

Luana nodded. "Your friend will probably be there anyway. Even if he isn't, we need to let the Protector know we've arrived on his island."

Luana scanned the sky. She put both hands to her mouth and made a high-pitched warbling sound. Joshua wondered what she was doing, but then a beautiful Kuela flew into view from over the palm trees. Luana extended her arm to one side. The magnificent bird circled above, then glided towards her and landed.

Luana gently stroked the bird's bright yellow beak. It cooed softly and ruffled its stunning plumage. She offered her cheek to the Kuela, and it stroked her face with the side of its long, yellow beak before extending its wings again and taking to the air. The magnificent bird circled once more before flying back over the palm trees again and out of site.

"Come," she said. "They'll be expecting us soon."

Luana led them off the beach and into the forest of palm trees. They walked for about half an hour before arriving at a clearing.

A man covered with tattoos on his arms and shoulders approached them. He raised his fist to his chest and bowed to greet them, smiling at Luana. "I was most pleased to hear of your arrival, Luana. Once again, you grace my island with your presence."

She beamed back at him. "Thank you, Protector. These are the strangers that arrived on Atoweena recently. This is Joshua, Andrew and Sarah."

The Protector bowed to each of them in turn. Luana turned to Joshua. "This is Alika," she said, gesturing to the man, "Protector of Kihala Island."

Luana turned again to Alika. "We've come to see the stranger who arrived here recently. Is he here?"

The man continued to look at Joshua and the others.

"This…guest of ours who arrived recently. He is…a friend of yours?" he asked Joshua.

"That's right," Joshua said. He stepped forward and bowed to greet the Protector. Joshua was unsure of the protocol and a little nervous but he could see that Alika was someone who was due the appropriate respect.

"Then perhaps he will listen to you more than he listens to me. Come this way."

The Protector led them into the centre of the village, where a big commotion was going on. A group of villagers stood in a circle looking at something. Although he couldn't see, Joshua recognised the unmistakable tone.

"Look, how many times do I have to tell you? Honestly!" came the voice from the centre of the throng.

"We have tried to reason with this…half-man," Alika said to Joshua, gesturing towards the circle of villagers, "but he refuses to believe anything we tell him."

The villagers fell silent and moved aside as they saw the imposing figure of their Protector leading Joshua and the others through.

"Galleon!" Joshua called out.

Galleon stood in the middle of the crowd with a look of irritation on his face. The Imp stopped his complaining and turned to them.

"Joshua? Andrew? Sarah? Finally! I've been trying to find out from these…" he paused and peered at the surrounding villagers before continuing in an angry and frustrated tone, "from these…*people*, where I am and how I got here but they keep going on about something called Archipelago."

"Galleon, what's the last thing you remember?" Joshua asked him.

The Imp took a deep breath and frowned a moment. "Well, I was with Andrew here. We were on the outskirts of Morelle waiting for you and Sarah to arrive and—" He paused. "Well, actually, I can't really remember much after that, to be honest. The next thing I knew, I was opening my eyes and staring up at a number of spears pointing and prodding at me like I was some sort of animal or something. They brought me here and I've been *trying* to reason with them ever since. What is this place? What are we doing here?"

"We think the Goat sent you here," Joshua explained. "Everyone else in Morelle is missing. The whole village is destroyed. We found Andrew on another island shortly after we arrived."

Galleon's jaw dropped. "The Goat? But I thought we killed him!"

"We did, too," Joshua said.

"So you just woke up and found yourselves here, as well?" he asked.

"Well, that's pretty much what happened to me," Andrew said.

"Sarah and I used the Orb of Sacrifice to get to this place," Joshua said. "Protello gave it to us before he died. It was his death that activated it."

"Protello's dead?" Galleon exclaimed. He stood there with his jaw open. "But…h-how?"

"We'll explain everything later," Joshua said. He turned to the Kihala Protector. "Alika, would it be possible for us to see the…Orb of Sunshine? I understand it's here on this island."

Alika pondered the question but said nothing initially. All the villagers also fell silent, waiting to see what their leader would say.

"The Orb of Sunshine is the most wonderful object," he said after a pause. "We are very proud of it. It is a precious gift of stunning beauty. What is your interest in the orb?"

"I think it might be able to help us get back home," Joshua said.

Alika narrowed his eyes. He turned his head towards Luana but still kept his eyes on Joshua. "Luana will take you to see the orb," he said finally. He turned his eyes to Luana, nodding. He turned back to Joshua and said, "You will take this…half-man with you." He gestured to Galleon.

Joshua wasn't sure whether that was a question or a command. "Um…yes, that is…if that's okay with you?"

Galleon raised his brow at Joshua.

"Good!" Alika said, in a definitive tone.

"Honestly!" An indignant look on his face, Galleon joined the others.

Luana raised her fist to her chest and bowed to Alika, who returned the gesture. Then she led them through the village and back into the forest of palm trees.

Christopher D. Morgan

# CHAPTER SEVEN
## *Kee'hea Nuts*

After walking for three hours, they found their way back to the coast but Joshua couldn't see the leaf boat they used to get to the island.

"What happened to the boat?" Andrew asked.

"Oh, it'll still be where we left it. We're much farther along the coast than where we arrived."

"Really? How can you tell? Everything looks the same to me."

"Look out there." Luana said pointing to some islands in the distance across the ocean. "That big island to the north is Atoweena."

"I don't remember seeing those other two islands over there to the west," Sarah said pointing in the direction of two islands to the left of Atoweena.

"That's right. They would have been behind it, just out of sight when we landed."

"Is that how you know where you are, by locating other islands?"

"That's one way." Luana nodded.

"Are the palm leaf boats how you normally get from island to island? Those things are amazing." Sarah was still grinning from ear to ear, taking everything in. "We don't have any islands where we're from. We have the River of Torrents, of course, and we do have the sea. But that's a long way from where I live. Galleon here, on the other hand, used to be a sea captain. Isn't that right, Galleon? Do your people travel between the islands a lot, Luana?"

Luana shook her head, grinning at Sarah's enthusiasm. "Most of the villages are inland. People tend to stay on the island they live on, by and large. Very few of us get to travel between the islands. It can be quite dangerous."

"How far is it to where the Orb of Sunshine is?" Joshua asked.

"Oh, it's quite far. We'll have to go tomorrow. It'll be dark soon and too dangerous to travel. It's up in the highlands."

"So, what on earth are we doing here, then? I'd hardly call it the highlands here at sea level. Honestly!" Galleon complained.

"I thought you might all be hungry," Luana said happily.

"You got that right," Andrew said with a beaming smile. "I'm starving."

"Did you say food?" Galleon blurt out with excitement, his face lighting up. It was the first sign of any positive emotion Joshua had seen from the Imp since they arrived in this world.

"Oh, I'd love to try some of the local cuisine." Sarah said to Luana. "What are we going to eat? There aren't any shrooms that I've noticed and I haven't seen any animals since we arrived."

"Plenty of those colourful birds, though," Andrew retorted. "Are they edible?"

Luana cast him a disapproving look. "Certainly not! There's our food," she pointed to the calm ocean water. She walked over to one of the palm trees and pulled another frond to the ground.

"Oh! Are we going to another island?" Sarah asked enthusiastically.

"Please don't say that," Andrew beseeched.

"No, not this time," Luana chuckled.

She knelt down beside the huge leaf and one by one, she tugged hard on the strands of thin fibre that extended from its sides. As she pulled each strand downwards from the leaf's outside edge, it sliced through the foliage, and a narrow strip of the green palm leaf came loose. She collected all the green strips into a pile and put them to one side. Then, she tied all the strands together, making one continuous line. She then tied one of the strips from the pile to one end of the long line of strands. Once tied, it formed the shape of a small butterfly.

Walking over to the water's edge, she swung the end of the line with the attached butterfly around her head twice before launching it out into the water. She then pulled it slowly back towards the shore again. As she pulled, the butterfly spun in the water, creating a shimmering effect.

"Is this how you catch fish?" Sarah asked with amazement.

Luana nodded. "They're attracted to the shimmering of the leaf as it spins in the water. The farther out we can throw the lure, the bigger the fish we can catch."

She pulled the line completely in but there was nothing attached to the butterfly.

"Can I try?" Sarah asked.

Luana raised her brow and shrugged but handed over the line and bait all the same. Sarah unhooked her slingshot and loaded the butterfly into the pouch. She pulled back hard and launched it out over the water. It went at least twice as far as before. Luana's jaw dropped and she tilted her head forward with her eyebrows raised. As Sarah pulled the line back in, she felt a tug on it.

"That's it," Luana said, clapping her hands gleefully, "just make sure you keep the tension on; otherwise you'll lose it."

Sarah's catch thrashed about as she lifted it out of the water and onto the beach.

"Wow!" Luana exclaimed happily. "That's a decent sized Opa'nu. Not bad for your first try."

The thrashing fish was about the length of a man's forearm. It was silver with yellow stripes down its length and a large dorsal fin sticking up from the top like a fan.

"Be careful of the fins, they're quite sharp."

Luana grabbed the fish, lifting it out of the water, still attached to the half-chewed sliver of leaf. She took some more leaf strips and expertly wrapped them around the fish until it was fully encased.

"Another couple like that and we should eat well," Luana said.

Sarah enthusiastically repeated the process and Joshua helped her haul in more of the Opa'nu, which, with Luana's help, they also wrapped in leaf strips.

"Me and Galleon will, um, go and find some firewood." Andrew suggested.

"Oh, that's okay. Here, watch." Luana said.

She walked back over to the same palm tree that she took the frond from, removed some dry pieces of tufty strips from its thick trunk and stacked them against each other in a pile on the beach.

"Right," she said, "I just need to light the fire."

Without further ado, she climbed up the trunk of the same palm tree. Reaching up through the leaves, she pulled out a cluster of white-petalled flowers with a small clump of red nuts in the centre and threw it to the ground.

"What's that for?" Sarah asked with keen interest. "They look very much like our Bramock"

"We call these Kea'hee nuts."

She discarded the white petals. Each nut had a strand attached to it. She separated one of the nuts from the clump and handed the others to Sarah, who watched intently. Luana then yanked down on the strand and tossed the nut into the pile of tufty strips. She stood up and backed away from the pile. Everyone else did likewise and they all watched in anticipation.

After a few seconds, there was loud crack and a puff of smoke emanated from the pile. The smoke was followed by small flames, which quickly took hold and the whole thing soon erupted into a roaring fire.

Their jaws dropped in amazement.

"Wow!" Joshua exclaimed.

"Is there anything these trees can't do?" Andrew said with a chuckle.

Luana just smiled. Once the fire had died down a little, she laid the wrapped fish onto the sides of the smouldering embers. Ten minutes later, they were steaming. Galleon was already licking his lips.

As the sun slowly set, the five of them sat by the crackling fire, enjoying the warmth. Luana deftly pried open the palm leaf strips, which now doubled as plates, and everyone enjoyed the steaming Opa'nu meat.

The sun had all but set by the time everyone finished their supper. With the fire still roaring and the gentle waves breaking over the sand, everyone sat in contemplation.

"You said you used the Orb of Sacrifice to get here?" Galleon asked Joshua.

"Hmm? Yes, that's right. Protello gave it to us. It activated as he died."

"Protello?" Luana asked.

"A friend," Joshua nodded. He gazed at the ground solemnly. "He saved my life on more than one occasion." There was a long pause. "But now he's gone."

Luana was listening keenly, taking it all in. "What happened?"

Joshua wanted to explain but couldn't quite find the words.

"How did he die?" Galleon asked, speaking for the first time since finishing his Opa'nu supper.

"We found him in Morelle. He was buried beneath a pile of burning embers. It must have been the Goat," Sarah said.

"Did he say anything before he died?" Galleon asked.

Joshua and Sarah caught each other's eye.

"He said I had to come here," Joshua said. He spoke slowly, as if in contemplation. "I have to open the next Portallas. He said I had to open them all."

"Open them all?" Andrew asked. "How many of them are there?"

Joshua shook his head and shrugged.

"He said I had to open all of them to be able to defeat the Goat. It was the last thing he said before he died. I think he was trying to tell me something else, too. He said I had to open all of the Portallas gateways before it was too late, or something." Joshua heaved a big sigh, shaking his head mournfully. "And then he was gone. It must have been really important but I don't know what it means."

"What do you suppose happens when all these Portallas gateways have been opened?" Andrew asked.

Joshua shook his head again.

"What's this Portallas thing?" Luana asked, looking at them each in turn. "What does it do?"

"We don't really know much about it," Sarah explained. "We know it's a gateway of some kind. Joshua opened one in Forestium, where we come from, when he brought three magical orbs together."

"And this friend of yours…Protello? He said you have to open the one here in Archipelago?" Luana asked.

Sarah nodded.

"How are you going to do this?"

Joshua pulled the Orb of Sacrifice from his keeper bag.

"You said the Orb of Sunshine looks like this," he said, passing the orb to Luana.

"That's right, although the markings on the side are different."

"Well, that's two orbs. Maybe there's a third one here in Archipelago somewhere?"

Luana slowly shook her head.

"I only know of the Orb of Sunshine."

"Never mind the orbs," Galleon retorted. "What about all the people from Morelle? Joshua, where's your mother and the others? Are they here somewhere? If so, where are they? Luana, do you know if there are any more people from our world here?"

Everyone turned to Luana. She shook her head.

"I don't know. Other than the four of you, I've not heard of any other outsiders showing up anywhere."

"Luana, could our people be on one of the other islands?" Joshua asked. "You said before there are lots of islands that you've never been to. Could my mother and the others be on one of those?"

Luana shrugged. "It's possible I suppose. But not much happens here that I don't get to hear about. The Kuelas usually see to that."

"The first thing we need to do is to find the Orb of Sunshine." Joshua said.

"Well, we should get some rest, then. It's a long journey to the highlands in the morning," Luana said, getting to her feet.

Much to everyone's further amazement, she demonstrated yet another use for the abundant palm leaves. She pulled a couple more from a nearby tree and tied them together back to back so as to form sleeping bags for each of them. Once it was clear what she was doing, everyone joined in to help her tie more of the palm fronds into sleeping bags.

After the sun had dipped below the horizon and the fire had simmered down, everyone found themselves getting very tired.

Joshua lay on his back and peered up into the sky through the open end of his comfortable sleeping bag. A pair of Kuelas soared across the sky in the moonlight. Their pleasant and intoxicating song together with the rhythmic sound of the waves gently breaking on the shore sent him swiftly off to sleep.

Christopher D. Morgan

# CHAPTER EIGHT
## *Orb of Sunshine*

Joshua awoke to tranquil waters glistening in the rays of the morning sun. Sitting up, he wiped his eyes to bring the world into focus again. Two of the other sleeping bags were already empty.

Joshua looked around. Luana approached from down the beach with Sarah. They were each holding a bunch of berries.

"Hungry?" Sarah asked, smiling as the two girls knelt down. The mere mention of food was enough to wake Andrew and Galleon, who both leapt out of their respective sleeping bags.

"Here," Sarah said enthusiastically. "Try these berries. They're unbelievably tasty! This place is amazing. There's such a huge number of new plants and trees and things. There's just so much to learn about this place. I could get lost here for months."

Joshua took one of the berries and bit into it. A smile spread across his face and he nodded his approval of the delicious treat.

After everyone feasted on the impromptu breakfast, Luana led them inland again.

"Is it much farther to the orb?" Joshua asked.

"Not really, but getting to the highlands means going over some rough terrain so we need to be careful."

It was indeed tough going, as they had to navigate uneven ground and thick vegetation. It would have been an easier if it weren't for the intense heat beating down on them.

As they climbed, the palm trees thinned out, which left them exposed to the heat of the sun, causing them to stop and rest frequently. Luana led the way, with Joshua close behind her. The others followed a short distance behind. They made their way up into the highlands over the course of the morning.

"You said before that you were an explorer?" Joshua asked Luana.

"Yes, that's right. I've explored more islands than anyone else I know on Atoweena. What's it like where you come from?"

"Forestium? Well, it's not quite as hot as here for one thing, and there are no islands as such. My people live in the forests."

"Forests?"

Joshua stopped to catch his breath and looked back over their trail. All of the trees he could see were palm trees, and most of those were not much taller than about twice his height.

"Those palm trees down there," he went on, "are those the only type of trees that you have here?"

"Well, yes, of course. Why?"

"In Forestium, we have lots of different types of trees and many of them are much taller than these I can see here. We make things from them. You know, from the different types of wood and vine and so on."

"Hmm. Doesn't sound that much different to here, really. The palms here provide us with most of what we need to live, day to day."

"That top you have on. It looks like it was also made from one of those huge palm leaves."

"Yes, I made it myself. Do you like it?"

Luana held out her arms in a pirouette as Joshua nodded his appreciation. Sarah watched, her eyes narrowed.

"Looks like Joshua is getting to know the natives," Galleon said as he held Sarah's hand to help her across a fallen palm tree.

"Hmm," she replied with a forced smile, "it does."

The sun was directly overhead before the terrain levelled out and the vegetation thinned. Luana led them to the top of a rocky outcrop with magnificent views out over the water in all directions. Joshua slowly turned full circle to take it all in. He could see the entire island from his vantage point.

Dozens of other islands dotted the ocean in all directions. Some were quite large but there were also lots of very small islands, some of which barely pushed up out of the water.

"Wow! There must be a hundred islands here," Andrew said.

"Over three hundred altogether," Luana said.

"How many of the islands are inhabited?" Sarah asked.

"Only twelve have permanent villages, but there are other islands that we stay on from time to time."

Just below them lay a rocky plateau, largely devoid of vegetation. In the centre there was a circle of trees. Luana pointed in that direction.

"That's where the sacred altar with the Orb of Sunshine is. But we need to be careful; those aren't ordinary palm trees."

"What do you mean?" Galleon asked. "They look just like all the others."

Sarah squinted into the distance, shaking her head slowly.

"No, the leaves are slightly smaller and the flowers are a different colour. I can see bulges on the trunks, also."

"Those are Pana'malu palms. If you disturb the leaves, they'll shoot toxic darts at you."

"Um, did you say something about...toxic darts?" Andrew asked. Luana nodded.

"It's a defence mechanism."

"Defence from what?" Galleon asked, now starting to look a little concerned.

"Palm Crabs. They like to eat the fruit at the top of the tree. We'll need to keep a sharp eye out for those too. The last thing we want is for one of us to be dragged off into the sea, or worse. Come on."

"Worse?" Galleon said to Andrew, as Luana continued walking. "What could possibly be worse?"

"Don't worry," Andrew dismissed. "I'm sure she's exaggerating. You stick with me and you'll be fine."

Luana walked on in the direction of the plateau. Joshua and the others shared a glance before following closely behind.

They crept towards the circle of Pana'malu palms, Luana vigilantly watching all around. There were a dozen of the strange trees. Like the palms they had seen elsewhere on the island, they had thick trunks and large green fronds drooping down to the ground. Each tree had fist-sized knots bulging out from around its trunk.

Through the circle of trees, Joshua saw a stone structure. It was ancient, overgrown with vines and lichen. The bottom section was composed of squared-off stones packed tightly together into a cube shape. Atop the cube was a round boulder.

Luana led them gingerly through the circle of trees and into the centre to where the altar stood. She was particularly careful not to disturb any of the palm fronds. The others all followed her lead, shifting sideways to avoid touching anything. This was difficult, as the trees were close to each other and there was very little space to walk between the dangling leaves.

Once inside the ring of trees, they walked around the altar. The boulder was flattened on one side, and recessed into the flat side was a spherical crystal. Joshua recognised it straight away. It was similar to the orbs he was already familiar with. Carved onto the side of the crystal was a circle with lines emanating outwards.

Luana knelt before the Orb. She lowered her head and muttered a soft incantation. When she was finished, she raised her head and gazed into the orb.

"Isn't it beautiful?" she whispered with a reverent smile.

"Why do your people worship the orb, Luana?" Sarah asked quietly.

"It is believed to have magic powers," she said, all the while admiring the orb.

"Legends tell of a time before there were islands here. The orb came down from the sun and the sun's rays shone through it. Where each ray of sunshine landed on the sea, an island appeared. Without the orb, our world would not exist; it is a precious gift to us from the heavens."

Joshua crept up to the orb to get a closer look. He slowly reached his hand out.

"Wait! What are you doing?" Luana screamed.

"This will help me to free my people, Luana."

"No, no!" she shook her head. "Nobody has ever removed the orb before. What if something bad happens?"

"It's just an orb," Andrew said. "Nothing bad is going to happen."

Joshua reached forward and took the clear crystal in his hand. As he did so, there was a clicking sound.

"What's that noise?" Andrew asked.

"Oh no!" Luana screamed, "PALM CRABS!"

Everyone spun around. It wasn't clear where the noise came from until Luana pointed towards one of the Pana'malu palms. From the behind it, a huge black crab emerged. Its body was the size of a full-grown wood-boar and it sported two huge claws that extended into the air. It had a spiny outer shell and long, jointed legs. Bright lights shone through the claws from two small eyes. One of the claws was rapidly opening and closing, making the clicking sound they could hear.

As they all huddled together, a second one, bigger than the first, emerged and it, too, made a clicking sound with one of its huge claws. It was quickly followed by a third and then a forth. In no time at all, the thorny beasts were bearing down on them from all directions.

Luana's eyes darted from tree to tree, trying to find an escape route. Joshua reached for his slingshot and launched a pebble at one of the creatures. The projectile struck the grotesque beast but just bounced right off the shell.

"No, that won't do any good!" Luana screamed. "We have to get out of here. NOW!"

She ran from the altar and everyone sprinted behind her. As they tried to weave their way between the trees, Galleon swiped one of the dangling palm leaves. Several swishing sounds followed, as darts from the bulges on the tree shot out in every direction.

As everyone fled the circle of trees, one of the darts struck Galleon in the side of his left leg and he screamed in agony.

# CHAPTER NINE
## *Ulaia Island*

After what seemed like an eternity of running, Galleon slowed down and insisted they stop and rest under a palm tree. Andrew kept a lookout but was unable to see or hear any of the spiny animals following them.

"Galleon! You're hurt!" Sarah cried.

A dart was still impaled in Galleon's leg and he was clutching at it, trying desperately to stem the flow of blood.

"I…I can't stop the bleeding."

"I'm afraid you won't be able to," Luana cried. "The poison prevents the blood from clotting. But that's not the only problem. We need to bind the leg tightly to prevent the poison from spreading. Otherwise—"

"Otherwise what?" Andrew asked.

"Otherwise…it will spread and…he won't survive. Quickly, help me with this!"

Sarah helped Luana pull one of the large palm leaves from a nearby tree. Just as she had done last night, Luana tore the leaf apart by pulling hard on the thin fibres that extended from its sides. Working as fast as she could, she soon had the strands loose. She tied them together and then bound Galleon's leg above where the dart was still impaled. Galleon screamed and arched his back in agony. The bleeding stopped.

"I'm sorry, Galleon. I have to remove the dart, but it will take some pulling."

"Why, won't it just come right out?" Andrew asked.

"No. It has barbs on the end. I'm sorry. This is going to hurt like hell."

She winced at Joshua and Andrew. "You'll have to hold him down for this."

Andrew and Joshua both gripped Galleon by the shoulders and braced themselves.

"Here," Luana rolled up one of the leaf strips, "bite down hard on this."

She stuffed it into Galleon's mouth as he continued to groan in agony. She nodded at Andrew and Joshua and said, "Ready?"

They both nodded back and leaned down hard on the Imp's shoulders. With a swift yank, she pulled the dart from Galleon's leg. The dart came out, tearing pieces of flesh along with it. The

Imp bit down hard on the palm leaf stripe, letting out a muffled scream. Then he collapsed to the ground. Blood oozed from the gaping wound.

Luana wiped the wound with another piece of palm leaf and bound it with more strips and more of the strands of fibre. Once it was bandaged, she leaned back against a rock and wiped her brow.

"I just hope we got it out in time."

"Come on, Galleon," Andrew said, "I know you can pull through."

"I'm not bloody dead yet, you blithering idiot!" Galleon screamed up at him.

Andrew chuckled. "Well, at least your charming disposition is still intact. Just don't get any ideas about dying now, do you hear me? Besides, I don't want to have to dig you a grave, even if it is only a small one!"

Galleon interrupted his whine of the agony with a grim chuckle. "Do you think I'm going to let you off easy?" he said, wincing, "I'll make you drag me across these islands first and *then* you can dig my grave."

"That's okay, you're only small, in case you'd forgotten."

"Not as small as your intellect."

"Bloody hell, aren't you dead yet?"

Everyone smiled as Galleon and Andrew continued bantering.

After a while, Luana stood up, pacing around.

"Why, Joshua? Why did you have to take the sacred orb? It's a bad omen to remove it from the altar. Look what's happened already."

"Well, we can't take it back now," Andrew said, "It's too dangerous. There's no way we'd get past those Palm Crabs and I don't fancy taking a chance with those toxic darts either."

Joshua turned to Luana and sighed. "I'm sorry, Luana. The orb is the only way I know to help us to find our people."

He shook his head. "Not only am I no closer to finding them, but now Galleon has been injured as well."

Meanwhile, in the grim confines of the Goat's dark room, His grotesque face contorted with rage as He paced back and forth. The vicious half-man, half-animal snorted and mumbled to himself. The hooves on His feet made a clicking sound as He strutted.

One of His forearms was missing. The end was shrivelled, like it had been burned. A piece of white bone poked through the flesh.

"It was him, I'm sure of it. But why is he here? I cannot allow him to open another Portallas. He must not find—"

The Goat roared and shook his head violently.

"You may have escaped my Blood-bats in Forestium, Joshua, but—"

The Goat stopped pacing, peered up into the dark, vaulted ceiling and howled.

Deep inside a dark cave the intermittent sound of clicks reverberated. One by one, pairs of lights lit up from dark corners. First it was a few, then more, and then dozens more. Before long, hundreds of pairs of lights were shifting left and right. The noise intensified.

Then a rumble echoed through the cavern, and the eyes in the dark scurried back into their corners. The cavern walls reverberate to a loud thumping noise. Rubble fell from the dark ceiling, trailing wisps of dust and debris. There was another thump, and another. The rumbling strengthened. The eyes in the dark continued to shift about.

From the depths of a dark tunnel, something huge approached. As it crept into the cavern, pairs of eyes scurried between its legs. Easily ten times the size of a human, the hideous beast raised its oversized pincers and clicked them open and shut repeatedly. The sound echoed through the caverns and soon hundreds of the smaller clicking sounds joined in the chorus. The horde of beasts was on the move towards the surface.

With each passing minute, toxin from the dart continued to spread throughout Galleon's system. Sweat dripped from his forehead as a fever took hold. His eyes rolled upward, showing bloodshot whites as his quivering arms flailed. His mutterings became increasingly incoherent.

"Luana, are there any herbs or other plants that can help Galleon?" Sarah asked, as she wiped his brow.

"Unfortunately, there's no known antidote to the darts."

"Surely there's something we can do?" Andrew pleaded.

"What happens if someone becomes ill here, Luana? Do you have medicines or doctors or something?" Joshua asked.

"Well, there are some plants that have healing properties, but once you've been hit by a toxic Pana'malu dart, there's usually nothing that anyone can do. Death often comes within a day or two."

They shared a glance and then looked down at Galleon, who by now was muttering gibberish to himself. He was sweating all over and shivering.

Luana let out a deep sigh.

"There is *someone* that might be able to help, but—"

Everyone stared at her.

"Who is it?" Joshua asked.

"We call him Kahu'niti. He's a…shaman…of sorts. He lives on Ulaia Island. It's…it's just that…" Luana shook her head, looking dejected.

"Just what?" Joshua asked.

"Well…he's a bit eccentric. People think he's mad. He talks in riddles a lot of the time. Most people are scared of him and prefer to let him be, but there have been stories in the past that he has healed people. I don't know if he can help, though."

"Well, we don't really have much to lose," Joshua conceded, "and we have to at least do something."

"Where is this Ulaia Island?" Andrew asked. "Can we get there in time?"

"It's not much more than a barren rock next to Kihala, where we are now. Kahu'niti lives there on his own, like a hermit. We can walk across the shallows to get there. We'll have to go now, though, if we're to make it there before high tide."

"Why is that important?" Andrew asked.

"The Mano'ana that live in the shallows come out then. It wouldn't be safe to cross when they are active."

Andrew raised his brow.

"Um…what are these…Mano'ana things? Some sort of fish?"

"More like an eel. They paralyse their prey with electric shocks. Not only is it painful but the stun effect can last long enough for you to drown. If you don't drown in that time, they will wrap around you to suffocate you to death."

Andrew, Sarah and Joshua all looked at each other and then at Galleon.

"Come on, then, we have no choice," Joshua declared. "We can't just sit here and wait for the toxin to kill him."

Sarah helped Luana build a makeshift stretcher and they laid Galleon onto it. Joshua and Andrew lifted one end and dragged it as Luana led them off in the direction of Ulaia Island.

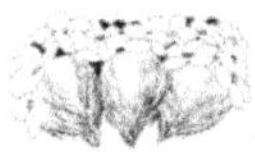

As they emerged from the thick vegetation of palms and onto the beach, they could see Ulaia Island out to the West. Bereft of any vegetation, the rocky island looked uninviting. If it weren't for the stretch of water between them, it might have been walking distance.

Luana pulled a couple of the huge leaves away from a nearby tree and they carefully laid Galleon onto them. With Luana and Joshua at the front, and Sarah and Andrew at the back, they eased Galleon's stretcher onto the water and floated it out towards the barren rock.

"Whatever you do, don't let go!" Luana said, as they set off across the shallows.

With the tide rising, it was becoming increasingly difficult to wade through the water. The evening twilight danced across the ripples, giving the illusion the sea was alive.

"What's that?" Andrew shouted. He pointed to dark shadows coming towards them. They were about half way across and by now wading in water up to their waists.

"Oh no!" Luana cried out. "Quickly! We need to hurry!"

Everyone picked up the pace, wading as fast as they could through the rising water. Joshua slipped and lost his grip on the palm frond. With nothing to support it, it sank into the water and a wave crashed over Galleon's face. He coughed and spluttered from inhaling the salty water. Luana held Galleon's head above the water again.

"Ouch!" Joshua screamed. "Something just stung me."

"Hold on! We're nearly there," Luana shouted.

Then Joshua felt another sharp jolt, like a bolt of lightning, strike his leg. His left side went numb and he fell into the water. He struggled to find his footing but he had no feeling in his left leg and found it difficult keep upright. Flailing his arms in the water, he felt another jolt and this time his entire body went stiff. Unable to move, he sank in the water, just managing to take in a lungful of air as his head submerged.

Joshua felt disoriented and wasn't sure which way was up. He opened his eyes to try to figure out where the surface of the water was but it was no use. Even if he could figure that out, he was unable to move any of his arms or legs.

The fast-moving current churned sand and seaweed all around him. He suppressed the urge to inhale for as long as he could.

Through the turbulent water, Joshua saw large objects swimming towards him. They had huge heads and long, winding bodies. One of them opened its jaw and Joshua could see rows of sharp, pointed teeth. The aggressive beast flexed its body and charged towards Joshua and high speed. Just as the eel was about to reach him, something came smashing through the water and struck the predator's slimy body. The Mano'ana writhed in pain and swam off.

Joshua felt he could hold his breathe no longer. As he opened his mouth to gasp for air, a hand pulled on his shoulder, lifting him out of the water. Joshua inhaled a lung-full of air, mixed with acrid, salty water.

"I've got you!" Andrew cried.

He lifted Joshua over his shoulder. With sensation beginning to return to his limbs, Joshua continued to cough and splutter as Andrew walked out of the water and laid his friend down onto the wet sand.

Sarah came over and held Joshua.

"You're very lucky to be alive, Joshua," Luana said. "I've never seen anyone attacked by three Mano'ana before."

Joshua sat up and caught his breath.

"Come on. We don't have time to lose. We need to find this shaman of yours."

Christopher D. Morgan

# CHAPTER TEN
## *Kahu'niti*

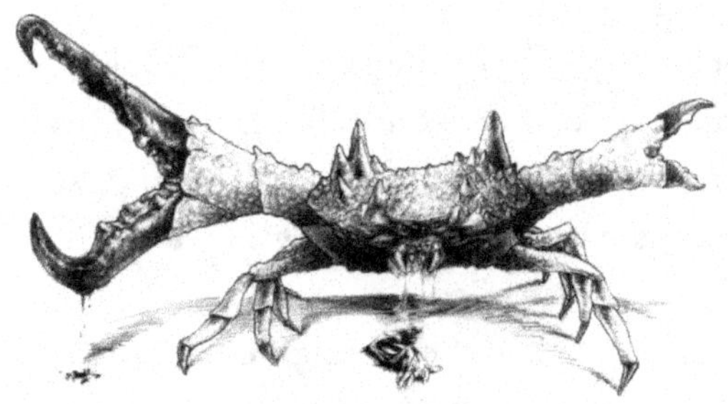

"Come on!" Luana pointed inland towards a wisp of smoke. "It's this way."

They each took a corner of the palm frond, raised Galleon off the ground and set off in the direction of the smoke.

After half an hour of struggling across the rocky terrain, they made their way to the entrance of a cave from which the smoke drifted.

"This is it," Luana said, and she led them all inside.

Although narrow and dark at first, the cave soon opened up into a cavern, with a fire crackling in the middle. It was difficult to see through all the smoke. A foul stench hung in the air.

They laid Galleon down close to the fire. He was shivering and no longer muttering. His skin was pale and clammy. Sarah knelt beside him and wiped his brow.

Joshua picked up a burning branch from the fire and held it out in front of him. He twisted around to get a better look of the cave. Suddenly, a figure stood before him.

"Beware the lights!" the figure shouted.

Startled, Joshua dropped the burning branch and stumbled backwards, falling to the ground. The figure strode over and stood before Joshua. It bent down over him and again shouted, "Beware the lights!"

In the flickering light of the fire, the silhouette of the scantily clad man was terrifying. He had a long, scruffy beard and matted hair. Tattoos covered his arms and shoulders. Joshua wasn't sure what to do and sat there, paralysed with fear.

"Kahu'niti?" Luana called.

The man turned to her, then straightened up. He tilted his head and widened his eyes.

"Luana?" He whispered.

"Yes, it's me. It's been a long time, my friend."

Kahu'niti shook his head and held his hands to his ears.

"No, no, no," he mumbled, "lights in the dark. She was too young. I didn't want to. I wasn't able to —"

He squatted down next to the fire, weeping.

"Such an innocent young girl. She was too young. Lights in the dark."

Sarah stood up and whispered to Luana, "What is it? Why is he so upset? What's he talking about?"

Luana heaved a big sigh.

"It's my sister," she said after a long pause. "Kahu'niti tried to rescue her from the attack when she was taken that night, but he was unable to save her. I don't think he's forgiven himself ever since."

The tormented Shaman continued muttering to himself.

"Kahu'niti, we need your help."

The shaman wept and rocked back and forth in front of the fire.

"Lights in the dark," he repeated, over and over.

"Kahu'niti! Please! You can't help Kalena anymore. But we need your help now."

The shaman stopped rocking and fell silent. Slowly, he lifted his head and stared at Luana, streets of tears visible down his face.

"My friend has been stung by a Pana'malu dart. He's…he's dying, Kahu'niti. Can you help him?"

Luana motioned to Galleon, who was still shivering and speaking gibberish quietly to himself.

Kahu'niti stood and walked over to Galleon. He took a burning branch from the fire and held it over the dying Imp's body. Moving it back and forth, he studied him closely. Stopping over the wound, he felt it with the palm of his hand before continuing. He reached for Galleon's forehead and felt it with the back of his hand. The shaman let out a deep sigh and stood up.

"There is nothing more to be done. The toxin has spread too far. I cannot help him now."

"What? No…no, wait, there must be something you can do for him?" Joshua pleaded, as he got to his feet.

"It is too late!" the shaman shouted. "The feather of green!"

"Feather of…what? W-what does that mean?" Joshua looked at Luana, shaking his head.

"Feather of green!" Kahu'niti repeated, pacing around the fire. "I cannot help, but the feather of green!"

Once again, he put his hands to his ears, shook his head and wept as he crouched down by the fire, rocking back and forth rhythmically.

"No more left. All gone now. Once there were many—"

Joshua looked pleadingly at Luana but she was unable to offer him any reassurance.

"I'm sorry. He's often like this," Luana sighed, looking down on the shaman pitifully. "Who knows what's going on in his mind."

Kahu'niti continued to speak in riddles.

"Too dangerous it is. He mustn't be found. Die he will if nothing is done. Beams of light!"

Joshua knelt beside Galleon and felt his dying friend's forehead. He put his head into his hands and heaved a big sigh.

"I wish I'd never heard of the Portallas…or the Goat."

Kahu'niti stood up and fixated at fire.

"Half man, half goat," he whispered, "killed them all."

Everyone turned to the shaman.

"Yes," Joshua said with widened eyes, his attention pulled into sharp focus. There was a renewed urgency in his voice as he looked at the crazy old man beseechingly. "The Goat. Do you know him? Please, you must help us."

Joshua felt a sense of hope for Galleon rising in his breast.

The shaman looked at him and then at the others in turn. He turned, walked deeper into the cave and out of sight.

"Where's he going?" Joshua asked Luana.

Before she could reply, the half-crazed man returned. He was holding something. Joshua couldn't quite see what it was at first but when Kahu'niti held it out over the light of the fire, Joshua could see it was a white feather.

"Feather of green," the shaman muttered and handed it to Joshua.

As he placed it into Joshua's hand, the feather slowly turned from white to green. The shaman gasped and jumped back.

"Joshua!" Sarah cried. "Could it be —"

As she said this, a sound from the front of the cave caught everyone's attention. It was a pleasant sound that Joshua remembered from when he first arrived. A colourful Kuela came gliding into the cavern. It sang a beautiful song and circled twice before landing next to Galleon.

Joshua and everyone else watched in stunned silence as the Kuela walked up to him. It peered into Joshua's eyes and then, without warning, grew taller. The bird's feathers shrunk, disappearing completely. Its entire body changed shape as it grew to Joshua's height. It morphed into a figure of a man.

"A…a Metamorph. You're a Metamorph!" Joshua said, excitedly.

"That's right, my friend. My name is Epani."

The Metamorph turned his attention to Galleon and knelt beside him. He held his hand over the Imp and moved it slowly back and forth the length of the dying man. A green glow emanated from Galleon's body. It lasted a few seconds and then subsided. When it did, Galleon slowly opened his eyes and looked around.

"Where…where am I?"

He peered up at Epani, who now stood up.

"And who the hell are you?" the Imp asked with resounding indignation.

"Sounds like he's well enough again." Andrew chortled.

Epani offered his hand to Galleon and helped him to his feet. Galleon pulled the strips of palm frond from his leg. The wound was gone and his leg was healed.

"What's going on here?" Galleon asked, as he shook his head in confusion.

"You are well now, my friend."

The Metamorph turned to Joshua.

"I cannot stay. It may already be too late. He has eyes everywhere in this world."

"Do you mean the Goat?" Joshua asked with wide eyes.

"Yes. You've heard of Him?"

Joshua nodded.

"We've heard of Him. He killed my father and we think he banished my people to this world. I'm here to rescue them. Do you know where they are?"

Epani surveyed the others in the cave before pacing by the crackling fire in silence. Everyone's eyes were trained on him. He stopped and turned to Joshua.

"The Goat is aware of your presence here, Joshua. You are in grave danger, my friend. I do not believe your people are here but if they were, they, too, would be in great peril. Even now, the dark forces of the Goat are on the move."

"Dark forces?" Andrew asked. "What are we up against?"

"A creature of great ferocity has been awakened by the Goat. I fear for all the people of this world."

"Do you mean those Palm Crabs?" Andrew asked.

"The Palm Crabs are creatures of the underworld. They are commanded by the Goat. What they see, He sees. The creature that the Goat has awakened, however, is much worse. I fear it may even be unstoppable."

"You said you don't believe my people are here," Joshua said. "Do you know where they are?"

Epani stared Joshua in the eye and sighed.

"You opened a Portallas before."

"Yes, in Forestium. H…how did you—"

"You must do so again…from this world."

"Why? What is the Portallas?"

"It is a gateway to the underworld, the realm of the Goat. Once opened, it cannot be sealed. The Goat is safe in his realm and cannot be harmed, but if the Portallas is opened, he is vulnerable. He will stop at nothing to prevent the Portallas from being opened."

"Are my people on the other side of the Portallas?"

"I believe that is where you will find them, Joshua."

"Protello also told me I had to open them all. It was the last thing he said before he died. But how do I open the Portallas from this world?"

"You have two orbs with you already, do you not?"

Joshua reached into his keeper bag, pulled out the two crystals and showed them to Epani.

"We have the Orb of Sunshine from Kihala," he said, showing Epani the crystal they had taken from the altar, "and this one," he went on, holding out the Orb of Sacrifice, "we got this one from…"

"You were given this from another Metamorph, from your world."

"Yes. How did you…"

"The Orb of Sacrifice was entrusted to Protello. His death was…necessary. Protello was the last of our kind from your world."

"Are there any other Metamorphs here in Archipelago?" Joshua asked.

Epani put his hand on Joshua's shoulder.

"I am the last of my kind here, my friend. If the Goat learns of my existence, I fear I will not be much longer for this world either."

"So, how do I open the Portallas from this world?"

Epani regarded the two orbs Joshua was holding and said, "There is a third orb. You will need to find it. The Oracle will guide you. You must—"

Suddenly, a clicking sound came from the front of the cave. It sent shivers down Joshua's spine.

"Beware the lights!" Kahu'niti blurted, leaping to his feet and pointing toward the sound. Two eyes lit up as the beast approached. Everyone stumbled as they tried scattering out of harm's way.

Epani morphed into a Kuela and took to the air. As he flew over the hideous crustacean, the vile creature reached high into the air, clipping the fleeing bird's tail feathers. The Kuela squealed, flapping its wings furiously as it struggled against the crab's vice-like grip.

"Quickly! Joshua!" Sarah screamed. "Do something!" She picked up a rock and threw it at the beast.

Everyone searched for something to use as a weapon. Joshua reached for a rock and hurled it at the thorny creature. Andrew and Galleon did likewise. The rocks struck the animal but simply ricochetted off its shell. The creature wasn't harmed but it was distracted enough to released its grip on the bird, which immediately flew out of the cave.

The Palm Crab raised its razor-sharp pincers above its head aggressively, its eyes lighting up. It scanned the cave, then turned to Joshua, who had stumbled to the ground. Joshua kicked furiously at the attacking animal as he tried desperately to push himself away. He still had the Orb of Sunshine in his hand and held it out instinctively to try to shield himself from the oncoming assault.

As the terrifying creature scuttled towards Joshua, the Orb in his hand pulsated. It flashed briefly, then erupted with bright shards of light.

Everyone shielded their eyes from the intense brightness. Beams of light shone out at the dark creature like sunshine. The brilliant streaks of light struck the menacing creature right in the eyes. It squealed and cowered, attempting to shield its eyes with its huge pincers.

After a few moments, the thorny crustacean stopped moving and collapsed under its own weight. The beams coming from the orb faded. Within a matter of seconds, the light had gone altogether and Joshua sat there staring at the crystal in his hand, his heart still pounding. The terrifying animal was no longer moving and its eyes no longer shone.

Everyone froze. Joshua felt his heart still racing in his chest. They all slowly got to their feet, staring at the motionless beast.

# CHAPTER ELEVEN

## *Under the Goat's Influence*

"Is…is it…dead?" Sarah whispered.

Luana got to her feet and crept over to the lifeless, black shell. Joshua also stood up and also went to check. Tentatively, he nudged it with his foot. It fell sideways. Both Joshua and Luana took a quick step backwards. The animal remained motionless.

"I think so," Joshua said. He peered at the Orb of Sunshine still in his hand.

"Well," Galleon said, getting onto his feet, "I can see why its brothers and sisters tried to attack us at the altar. I can't imagine them wanting anyone to get their hands on that thing."

Joshua nodded at him.

"But what about Epani?" Andrew said. "Wasn't he saying something about a third orb?"

"Yes," Sarah said. "That's right. He said the Oracle will guide you in finding it."

"Luana, do you know of the Oracle in this world?" Joshua asked.

"Oracle? Well, I…I don't know. I've never heard of an Oracle. What is it?"

"Well, in Forestium, it's a wise being that took the form of a flame."

"Oh, well, I don't know about an Oracle but you might be talking about the Flame of Eternity."

"Flame of Eternity?" Sarah asked.

"Yes. Well, it's only a legend, of course. It's said the Flame of Eternity will grant you knowledge of the future. Anyway, nobody knows where the flame is and I've never come across it. I don't think it even exists."

"Beware the lights," Kahu'niti whispered. He crept over to the fire again and rocked back and forth rhythmically.

"Beware the lights," he mumbled. "Last of his kind. Once there were many. Flame of Eternity —"

"Actually," Galleon said, "I'm starting to think this crazy old man is smarter than the rest of us put together. Maybe he knows where the Oracle is."

"Kahu'niti?" Luana said softly, sitting beside him and taking him gently by the arm. The troubled man stopped rambling and fell still. "Do you…know where the third orb is, or where we can find the Flame of Eternity?"

The Shaman sat there momentarily before turning to Luana. He started whimpering again. "Such a sweet little girl," he cried, shaking his head slowly. "Wasn't fair. She shouldn't have died." A tear welled in his eye and he began to sob. "I couldn't help her. I couldn't stop it. I wasn't strong enough to—"

Luana put her arms around him and held him warmly. "Shhh," she said softly, "I know, it's all right."

After a few moments, Luana released him and stood up. Turning to the others, she said, "It's no use. I don't think he can help us."

"Okay, well now what?" Andrew sighed. "You said there were hundreds of islands here. It'd take us forever to find the third orb. There must be some way to narrow it down?"

Joshua paced back and forth.

"Luana, didn't you tell us that Kuelas can read your thoughts?"

"That's right. Why?"

"Well, couldn't you ask one of them to help us locate the Oracle?"

She pursed her lips and pondered this for a moment. Shrugging her shoulders, she said, "I guess I could try. Come on, let's leave Kahu'niti in peace."

"Well, how are we going to get off this island? I don't fancy another run-in with those Mano'ana things," Joshua said.

"Well, there's a boat on the northernmost beach here. We can use that to get across to Kuela's Nest Island."

Luana gave the Shaman a tender kiss on the forehead and led the others out of the cave.

Kahu'niti sat in his cave for quite some time after the others had left. He rocked back and forth in front of the fire, mumbling to himself.

After a while, he crept towards the lifeless creature. Kneeling down in front of it, he peered at the grotesque animal.

It was black all over and covered with sharp thorns protruding from its tough, shiny shell.

The Shaman stared pensively into the creature's eyes. He could see the flames glinting off them like a reflection in a mirror. After a while, a strange sensation overcame him. The dancing flames from the fire cast eerie shadows on the cave walls, and he felt himself drifting into a trance. The crustacean's eyes lit up. The brighter they became, the more Kahu'niti's trance deepened. He wanted to react but felt powerless to do so.

He felt himself floating in a dark place, as if disconnected from his body. It was disorienting at first and he struggled against his own confusion at what was happening to him.

Then, as the fog was clearing in his mind, a dark swirl formed in the distance. It raced towards him, getting bigger and bigger, like he was moving through a tunnel. The swirl continued to get closer, filling his field of vision. It twisted and contorted, slowly taking form. It was like a dark cloud descending on him. When it was right up to his face, the cloud evaporated, leaving the image of a dark, horned man. It was the Goat.

Kahu'niti's immediate reaction was one of deep loathing and unrestrained terror.

"N…no! Not again. Why? Why do you do this to me? I've done all that you have asked of me. Please! I beg you. Release me from this torment."

A hideous grin formed across the Goat's face.

"All in good time, perhaps. But first there is something else I need you to do."

"No. No more. Please! I will not help you again."

The Goat cackled and lowered His head. The foul creature's dark eyes peered through His bushy brow as He leaned forward. His ribbed horns extended from either side of his head.

"You did well to kill that little girl when I commanded you to do so. Now you will kill another. The boy that seeks the orbs."

"No! I won't do it. You can't make me do it. Please, I beg you, I don't want to kill anyone. I never wanted to kill anyone. Don't torture me by making me kill again." Kahu'niti sobbed in anguish. "Please! I'll do anything you want, don't make me kill again."

The Goat roared and shook His head violently. The sound pierced through Kahu'niti's mind like a sharp knife slicing at a wound.

"You will kill the boy, or I will make you kill them all. And when you are done killing every last man, woman and child, you will have to live with that knowledge."

The Goat leaned closer and widened His eyes. Bright beams of light shone from them into Kahu'niti's eyes.

Without wanting to, Kahu'niti took a sharp intake of breath and his eyes opened wide. He tried to resist looking at the lights boring into him but he was utterly at the Goat's mercy.

With full control over what He wanted Kahu'niti to think and feel, the Goat's eyes flashed and Kahu'niti felt a burning sensation, like the light from the Goat's eyes were beaming straight into his soul.

"This will help you kill the boy."

The Goat roared and shook His head violently. The sound echoed throughout Kahu'niti's mind, sending the tormented soul's anguish higher still, before fading. As it did, an object formed in Kahu'niti's hand.

Just as he thought he could endure it no longer, the sound faded and the image before him disappeared from the outside in, like a collapsing vortex. Eventually, all that remained were the lights of the Goat's eyes staring back at him.

After a few seconds, the vision cleared and the image of the lifeless Palm Crab came back into view. Kahu'niti was now staring at the animal's eyes shining back at him. They faded until they went out altogether.

Panting from his ordeal, Kahu'niti stood up and peered across the dark cave with a sense of purpose. He looked down. There was something in his hand—something that wasn't there before. He raised it to his face to study it in the light of the fire. It was a dagger. The blade was about half the length of his forearm and it had a vicious-looking, serrated edge on one side. As he twisted it to get a good look, the reflection of light from the fire lit up his face briefly. It revealed an expression of determination.

He gripped the handle and leered at the thorny crab. Then, he hastened out of the cave and was gone.

# CHAPTER TWELVE
## *The Attack*

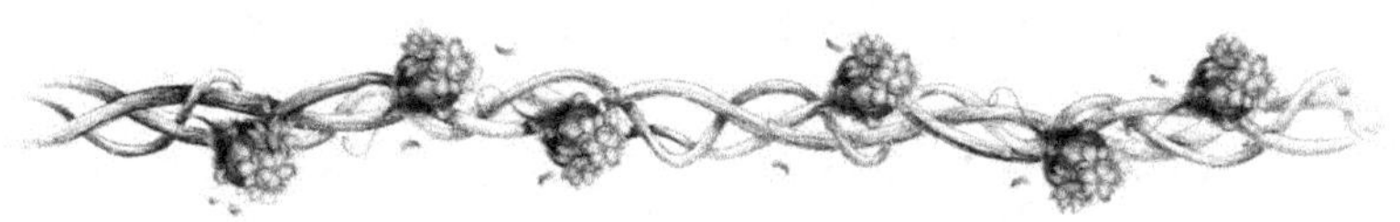

The sun was setting by the time Luana brought the four of them to the northwest coast of Ulaia. The warm evening sea breeze felt pleasant on Joshua's arms and face. Long shadows trailed them as they walked along the beach.

Galleon became increasingly frustrated as he struggled, the soft sand shifting beneath his feet.

"Where are we going now?" he called out, impatiently. "Honestly, how can you people walk on this sand? Every time I take a step forward, I end up slipping half a bloody step back. It's hard going and it's getting everywhere. I've had more fun pulling out ingrown toenails than walking through this stuff."

"We're going to Kuela's Nest Island," Luana said, turning to him with a hint of a chuckle.

"Great!" he said, mumbling to himself. "That's all I need, a trip across choppy waters infested with those damned eel things. And I was just thinking I hadn't nearly died enough already over the past couple of days. Honestly!"

"What's that?" Luana asked.

"Oh, nothing," he lied.

Luana rolled her eyes and said, "Well, why don't you just take those boots off? It'll be much more comfortable."

Galleon stopped and stared at his feet.

"You said you're taking us to Kuela's Nest Island?" Joshua asked.

"What's there?" Andrew asked.

"What do you mean, what's there?" Galleon retorted with a chuckle. "A bloody holiday camp maybe? Kuelas, you idiot."

"Okay, okay, keep your hair on. I meant what are we going to be doing there," Andrew said, shooting Galleon an indignant look.

"There's a colony of Kuelas that nest there. If we are going to try to find the Oracle, we'll need as much help as we can get."

"Hold up!" Galleon shouted. He had been removing his boots and was now some distance behind them.

Everybody stopped and waited. As they stood and watched Galleon, a figure appeared in the distance, back along the beach. It started trotting towards them. Luana squinted but the setting sun made it difficult to make out who it was.

"Kahu'niti?" she muttered to herself. "That's odd. He hardly ever leaves his cave."

"Maybe he wants to help us find the Oracle?" Joshua suggested.

Kahu'niti sped up and was now sprinting towards them. Galleon had just stood up and was brushing himself down when the Shaman ran past him, pushing him to the ground in the process.

"Something's not right." Luana said.

"What's that in his hand?" Andrew asked.

Kahu'niti ran straight at Joshua, eyes fixed on him. As the Shaman got closer, he raised a dagger and was poised to thrust it at the young Woodsman. Joshua stepped backwards but stumbled on the sand, falling to the ground. Kahu'niti lunged at Joshua, letting out a roar as he thrust the dagger down.

At that moment, a Kuela came swooping in and collided with the Shaman. It grabbed at his face with its talons, flapping its wings furiously. Andrew rushed in and tried to wrestle the dagger out of Kahu'niti's hands but was unable to break it loose.

Luana grabbed the shaman's arm and shouted, "Kahu'niti, no!"

Kahu'niti fell to the ground, trying to pull the flapping Kuela away from his face. Joshua got to his feet and they all ran off the beach and into the forest of palm trees, leaving the shaman writhing on the sand trying to fend off the attacking bird.

They ran for several minutes before stopping to catch their breaths.

Panting heavily, Joshua said, "What was that all about?"

"I don't know," Luana said, struggling to catch her breath. "I've never seen him behave that way before."

"He…he seemed possessed or something. If it wasn't for that Kuela, I'm pretty sure he would have killed me."

"Joshua!" Sarah gasped. "Your arm! It's bleeding?"

Blood dripped from Joshua's hand as it trickled down his arm.

"It's nothing, just a scratch. I've had worse."

"Better let me take a look at it all the same," Sarah insisted. "We don't want it getting infected."

"Where's Galleon?" Andrew asked, as Sarah tended to Joshua's wound.

Everyone scanned the area but the Imp was nowhere.

"I'm sure I saw him running towards us," Sarah said. "He might have gone after Kahu'niti. He can't be far. Maybe we should spread out and look for him?"

"But what about Kahu'niti?" Andrew asked. "He's still out there somewhere."

"Andrew's right," Joshua said. "It's safer if we stick together."

"Ouch!" a voice shouted from somewhere in the distance. "Bloody shells! Honestly!"

"Galleon!" Andrew whispered as loudly as he could. "Over here!"

A few seconds later, Galleon waddled in through the thick underbrush, barefoot and limping. Everyone heaved a sigh of relief.

"Great!" the Imp said. "To top everything else off, now we have a deranged madman on the loose chasing us. Honestly! This place is really starting to get on my nerves."

"Chasing *me*, you mean," Joshua said.

"Yes, that did seem to be the case," Galleon said. "I wonder what set him off?"

"I don't know. It isn't like I did anything to upset him." Joshua thought for a moment. "Hold on. Didn't Epani say something about the Goat knowing I was here?"

"That's right," Sarah said. "He also said the Goat's dark forces were on the move."

"Well, maybe the Goat was behind it. Maybe Kahu'niti is acting under the Goat's influence."

"If that's the case, we need to get you as far from here as possible, in case he comes after you again," Andrew said.

Joshua nodded. Turning to Luana, he said, "How far is it to Kuela's Nest Island?"

"Once we reach the northern tip of Ulaia, it's not that far by boat. If we hurry, we can make it there by nightfall. We'll have to make camp for the night and cross over in the morning."

"Come on then," Joshua said. "We shouldn't waste any time. Hopefully, we can avoid any more surprises."

Everyone followed Luana as she led them through the underbrush in a northerly direction.

"Ouch!" Galleon shouted. "Bloody shells!"

It was dark by the time they reached the boat on Ulaia's northern coast. It was a cloudless night with moonlight glistening over the calm waters. There was a soft sea breeze but the air was still humid. Gentle waves broke over the beach with a comforting sound. Joshua could make out the silhouette of another island on the horizon.

"We'll camp here for the night," Luana said. "I'll get the fire going up there in the trees, where it's out of sight."

"I'll have a go at catching some fish," Sarah suggested.

"Come on, Andrew," Joshua said, "let's see if we can make some of those comfortable sleeping bags."

"Well, I'm just going to plonk myself down," Galleon scoffed. "My feet are bloody killing me."

With that, he sank onto the soft sand in a heap. He lay back, stretched his arms out beside him and let out a satisfying sigh.

Before long, Sarah managed to catch a couple of decent sized Opa'nu, which Luana wrapped and cooked on the fire. Everyone ate well, although nobody spoke much. It had been a very tiring couple of days and everyone was exhausted. Once they had all finished eating, Luana kicked sand onto the fire to put it out and suggested that everyone get some rest for the night.

Joshua and Andrew sat by the dead fire after the others had tucked themselves in. Joshua waited for several minutes until he could hear the others snoring.

"I think I'm in trouble," he said, nudging Andrew.

"Hmm? What do you mean?"

"I mean…Luana. I, um…I think she's taken a liking to me."

"So? What's the problem?"

"Sarah, obviously," he said, slapping Andrew with the back of his hand. "I mean, of course Sarah knows I have no interest in Luana but…I don't know. I just don't want to upset Luana's feelings. What do you think I should do?"

Andrew shrugged. "Why don't you just come out and say something to her? Make sure she understands you're taken."

"She's not bad looking," Joshua said, raising his eyebrows suggestively at Andrew.

"What, me? And Luana?" Andrew shook his head, chuckling. "No thanks, mate. I've already got enough on my plate trying to keep you alive. Besides, you've already tried setting me up once before with Isabelle, remember? Look how well that turned out. No, you're on your own there I'm afraid."

Joshua sighed. "I just hope she doesn't get hurt, that's all."

"Look, you've got more important things to worry about for the moment. You get off to sleep, mate. I'll keep watch for a few hours. That madman is still on the loose somewhere on this island. Don't worry, I'll try to keep you alive for just little longer."

Joshua chuckled. He stepped into his palm-leaf sleeping bag and reflected on the events of the day. Between worrying about where his people were, whether he would find the Oracle and the third Orb, how to open the Portallas, sneak crab attacks in the middle of the night and now Kahu'niti out looking for him, it was going to be a long and possibly restless night. But at least he had his friend watching out for him. With that comforting thought, he drifted off to sleep.

# CHAPTER THIRTEEN
## *Eyes for Joshua*

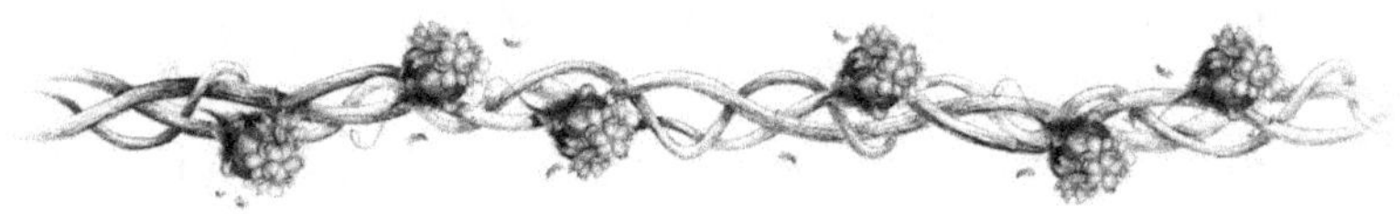

Joshua opened his eyes to see smoke rising from the burnt embers of last night's fire. There was a chill in the air. He could see the steam from his breath each time he exhaled. Dark clouds were brewing and the previously gentle waters were now tumbling with white crests. A storm was closing in.

A sickening feeling of dread overcame Joshua when he remembered the attack from Kahu'niti last night. He sat up to check on everyone. All the sleeping bags were still occupied. The sound of the waves breaking over the beach wasn't quite loud enough to drown out Andrew and Galleon's snoring. Luana was stretching her arms. She slipped out of her sleeping bag and stood up, yawning. She looked down at Joshua and smiled.

Joshua stood up and peered out over the water to the nearby Kuela's Nest Island. He could see it more clearly now that the sun was up. It didn't seem as big as Ulaia. The small island jutted with sheer cliffs and rocky ledges. Several dozen Kuelas were coming and going, buzzing around the island like flies.

"So, where's this boat?" Joshua asked.

"Not far from here. Come, let's go and find something to eat before the others wake."

Joshua and Luana strolled along the shore until they found a cluster of bushes at the boundary of the beach and the tree-line.

"Those look like the same berries we had the other day," Joshua said.

"That's right. Just make sure you only pick the red ones. The paler ones aren't ripe yet and will taste sour."

They both plucked the berries from the bushes. Joshua had collected a handful when Luana paused and turned to him.

"How long have you known Sarah?"

"Not very long," Joshua said, standing upright with his hands cupped full of the red fruits.

"Do you think she's the right woman for you?"

Joshua froze momentarily, wondering whether he had heard Luana correctly.

"W…what? W-what makes you ask?" he stammered, shaking his head.

"I think the right woman for you would be more…attentive. I would think she'd take more of an interest in you."

Joshua opened his mouth then pursed his lips as if to say something, but his face froze in that position not knowing how he should respond.

"You know…you could consider remaining here in Archipelago," she said, smiling at him.

"I…well, I mean—"

"Hey, I thought you'd like a hand," Sarah said, walking up to them both. Joshua turned, startled by Sarah's sudden appearance. Sarah leaned towards him and gave him a quick kiss on the cheek. "Want a hand?" she said.

"Um, yes. We're, um…you know…we're just…picking berries. Aren't we, Luana?"

Luana smiled at Sarah. "I think we have enough now. Come on, I'm sure the others will be hungry by now."

Luana walked off.

"We'll be right there," Joshua said with a smile.

"Look…" he said. He wanted to tell Sarah about his dilemma with Luana but she cut him off.

"I think she likes you," Sarah said.

"Um, really?"

"Oh, come on, Joshua. I'm sure you've noticed it by now."

Joshua sighed. "I don't know what to do. She must know that we're a couple, surely?"

Sarah thought for a moment. "Well, she probably idolises you a little. I'd just be careful about saying or doing anything to encourage that further. Who knows what sort of customs these islanders have? For all we know, just talking to her might be interpreted as you taking an interest in her."

"Hmmm. You might be right."

Sarah smiled. Giving him a peck on his cheek, she said, "So long as you remember you're still all mine, you'll be fine." She then turned and led him by the hand back to the others.

Back at the camp, Andrew and Galleon were now awake. Andrew had lit the fire again, and it was already roaring. Galleon was rubbing his hands together over the flames.

Joshua dropped his armful of berries onto those Luana had already piled on a palm leaf, and they all sat and ate. Joshua didn't say anything. Luana kept looking him in the eye. Sarah was glancing back and forth between Joshua and Luana. Andrew and Galleon were both too busy eating berries to notice anything.

"Doesn't look too far to that island," Galleon said. "Please tell me I'm right."

"I quite liked the boat ride from the other day," Joshua said, chuckling. "That was exhilarating."

"Hmm. Yes, well I'd like to hold on to my breakfast for a little bit longer, thank you very much," Galleon scoffed. "I've never been very good on the water."

Andrew chuckled. "And that coming from the man that made his living on a boat for all those years? How on earth did you manage?"

"That was over ten years ago. I've long since lost my sea legs."

"Yes, don't worry, Galleon," Luana said. "The wind is heading in the right direction so it shouldn't be a long ride."

Joshua stood up. "Come on. The sooner we leave, the sooner we'll get there."

"The boat is over here. Just watch out for these sharp reeds in the sand."

"Ouch!" Galleon shouted. "Blimey. Now I wish I'd kept my boots after all. I can't bloody win, here!"

"What happened to your boots, Galleon?" Sarah asked.

"Probably still on the beach on the other side of the island. I must have left them there when that madman attacked Joshua yesterday evening."

"I wonder what happened to him?" Andrew asked. "I mean that Kuela was really tearing into him."

"He could be anywhere," Sarah said.

"That's right," Joshua said. "All the more reason we should get off this island as soon as we can."

Just along the beach, they found the boat Luana had been telling them about. It was little more than a dozen logs strapped together with a simple mast and a sail made from dried palm fronds. They all lifted the boat into the water, wading out to about waist deep before climbing on.

"Here, grab these," Luana said, pointing to wooden paddles. Joshua and Andrew took one each and paddled the raft through the water. Luana steered with a rudder at the back. The tail wind helped blow them towards the distant island.

Galleon sat on the front and dangled his feet in the water.

"Ouch!" he shouted, lurching backwards, rubbing his feet. "What was that?"

"Just make sure to keep your arms and feet out of the water," Luana shouted from the back. "You don't want to get stung by a Mano'ana."

"Now she bloody tells me," Galleon scoffed, getting to his feet and moving to the very centre of the raft. "Honestly!"

Just as Luana predicted, the ride over to Kuela's Nest Island was a brief one, taking them about twenty minutes. When they reached the shallows, Luana jumped into the water at the front and pulled the raft close to the beach.

"Okay, you can all get off now. Just watch out for the urchins here in the shallows. Don't step on any whatever you do."

They all followed Luana's lead and jumped into the water. Everyone managed to avoid the spiny urchins. Well, almost everyone.

"Ouch! Bloody urchins!" Galleon shouted.

# CHAPTER FOURTEEN
## *Kuela's Nest Island*

After pulling the raft up onto the beach, Joshua took in his surroundings. Far fewer palm trees grew on this rocky island. The white, sandy beach gave way to outcroppings of huge boulders. Dozens of brightly coloured Kuelas soared above them, swooping back and forth on the thermal updrafts coming in from the shore. The air was full of the sound of birds singing. It was pleasing, like a lullaby.

"Wow! Just look at them all!" Sarah gushed. "They look and sound just beautiful. There must be…hundreds of them. We have birds where we're from but we never see them in these numbers. Is this the only place where they nest? What do their eggs look like? They're sort of like Raetheons. Well, not really. I mean I suppose they're birds of course, but—"

"Ahem," Andrew said, interrupting Sarah's runaway enthusiasm. "The sooner we find the Oracle, the better, right?"

"Come on," Luana said, smiling, "they tend to nest in the centre of the island. That's where we'll find the biggest concentration of them."

"Luana, how is it you can communicate with the Kuelas?" Joshua asked, as he caught up and walked beside her.

"Well, we just do. I don't really know how. I've never thought that much about it, to be honest. Don't you talk to your animals where you come from?"

"Talk to animals?" Galleon scoffed. "You say that like it's the most normal thing in the world. We can't talk to animals in Forestium. I can barely talk to some people. If I tried chatting to a Wood-boar, I'd probably be locked up. Besides, I can hardly understand my own thoughts sometimes, much less those of wild animals."

Luana shrugged and smiled at him.

After about half an hour of trekking, Luana led them to the edge of a natural basin at the centre of the island.

"Come on," she said, "it's just over that last ridge."

As they made their way up to the final ledge, they peered over and into the caldera below. Joshua's jaw dropped. Hundreds, if not thousands, of Kuela nests littered the landscape as far as the eye could see. They were in the trees, between rocks and even right there on the ground. Each nest was constructed from an assortment of leaves, twigs and feathers. Many were occupied by one or two Kuelas, but some were empty.

"Hey look," Andrew exclaimed, pointing at one nest in particular. Two speckled, yellow eggs rested in the middle of the next. "Are those eggs edible?"

"Certainly not!" Luana said, scolding him with a frown.

"So, what now?" Joshua asked.

"Wait here," Luana said.

She walked down into the basin, towards the middle of the caldera. None of the Kuelas appeared to take much notice of her, initially. There was a pile of boulders in the centre, onto which she climbed.

As everyone else watched with amazement, Luana held out her arms, raised her head and closed her eyes. Before long, some of the Kuelas took to the air and flew in circles around her. They were soon joined by others. Within seconds, hundreds of the beautiful birds encircling the young woman. They flew faster and faster, until a vortex formed around her.

Luana kept her arms outstretched with her palms face up. The wind from the vortex blew so strongly it sent twigs and feathers flying in all directions.

Then the Kuelas veered away from her, flying off in all directions. After a few seconds, they had all disappeared and an eerie quiet descended on the island. The pleasing lullaby sounds were gone and the only remaining noise was the gentle rush of breeze rustling through the trees. A few stray feathers floated to the ground.

Luana lowered her head and opened her eyes. She looked around, stepped down from the boulders and walked back over to the others.

"Luana, that was amazing. What just happened?" Joshua asked.

"I asked them to help me find the Flame of Eternity," she replied.

"Okay, so…what happens now?"

"Now…we wait. We might as well make ourselves comfortable. It could be some time before they return."

"Well, if we're going to be here a while," Andrew said, "we should have something to eat. Are you sure those eggs aren't edible?"

Luana tutted. She pointed to the far side of the caldera. "If you walk in that direction, there are some Lili'kio fruit trees. Make sure you pick the red ones, though. The green ones will taste bitter."

"Come on, Galleon," Andrew said. "Let's go see what these Lili'kio things taste like."

"Oh! I'll come with you," Sarah said. "I'd love to explore the island some more." She leaned over to Joshua and gave him a kiss on the cheek, saying, "We won't be long, okay?"

As they walked off, Sarah glanced over her shoulder at Joshua and blew him another kiss.

Joshua was about to say he was going to join them but Luana cut him off.

"You and I can stay here and get a fire going then, Joshua."

"Um…okay. Yes, I…I guess that's fine," he said with a touch of nervousness. "Um, don't be too long now," he shouted out to the others. But they were already making their way across the basin and were soon out of sight.

For the next few minutes, Joshua busied himself with gathering some dried twigs and things for a fire. Luana found a small bunch of Kea'hee nuts and used them to set the tinder alight. Even though it wasn't comfortable, Joshua found a spot on the opposite side of the fire to Luana and took a seat. An awkward silence descended.

"I, um…I wonder what happened to Kahu'niti," Joshua said as the silence was becoming uncomfortable.

"Hmm? Oh, yes, I've been wondering that myself. I really don't know what got into him. He's never done anything like that before."

"Maybe all that time living alone?"

"Perhaps."

"I wonder why he came after me…specifically, I mean."

"Well, you did take the Orb of Sunshine. That's a sacred thing to my people."

Joshua lowered his head and said nothing for a few moments.

"I just don't know any other way to open the Portallas," he said, shaking his head. "In Forestium, I opened the gateway by bringing three orbs together. Epani said I had to do the same in this world also."

Luana said nothing yet continued to stare at him. Joshua tried to figure out what she was thinking but her expression wasn't giving anything away.

"Back in the cave, on Ulaia," Luana said with a thoughtful frown, "when you were talking to that Metamorph, you said something about another Metamorph from your world?"

"Protello?"

"Yes, that's it. You said he was trying to tell you something…before he died."

"Hmm. He said I had to open the Portallas. I had to open them all…before it was too late."

"Too late for what?"

"I…well, actually, I don't know."

The two of them sat in silence for the next few minutes. Joshua prodded the fire with a small branch he'd been toying with.

"She could pay more attention to you, you know," Luana said.

Joshua froze, his eyes shifting left and right. "Um, s-sorry?" he said.

"Here, we pay much more attention to our partners. If I had someone like you, I'd pay much more attention to you."

"W-what do you mean?"

Luana eyed him with an enigmatic smile. Joshua opened his mouth to speak but couldn't find the words and his jaw hung there.

"Lili'kio fruits anyone?" Andrew, Galleon and Sarah came wandering back, dropping an armful of the fruits to the ground by the fire. Andrew handed one to Joshua. "Here you go mate, you should try them. They really are quite delicious."

Joshua looked at Luana, but she got up and broke eye contact with him. He glanced at Andrew and shook his head slightly, as if to decline the offer of the fruit.

Andrew shrugged and took a bite out of the fruit himself.

"Really, Andrew? How many of those have you eaten already? Honestly!"

"Hey, I'm hungry. What can I say? Besides, these things are delicious."

"So," Sarah said, sitting beside Joshua. "This place is amazing. There are so many new plants and fruits here. I could see myself spending months exploring all the islands. Have any of the Kuelas returned yet?"

Joshua opened his mouth to speak when Andrew blurted out with excitement, "Hey, look! There they come now."

Everyone glanced up. A few Kuelas flew into the basin. They circled a couple of times before floating down towards the ground, each finding a nest.

"Hmm. Doesn't look like those ones found anything," Luana said.

"How do you know?" Sarah asked.

Before Luana had a chance to respond, more Kuelas came flying in. They also circled. All of them landed except one. It glided over to the fire and flapped its wings above them. Luana held out her arm and it landed there gracefully. The Kuela rubbed its long, yellow beak on Luana's cheek.

"That one certainly seems to know something," Galleon said.

The Kuela took to the air again and circled above the fire. It squeaked and then flew off.

"Come on," Luana said, excitedly. "It's found something. Quickly, or we'll lose it."

# CHAPTER FIFTEEN
## *The Flame of Eternity*

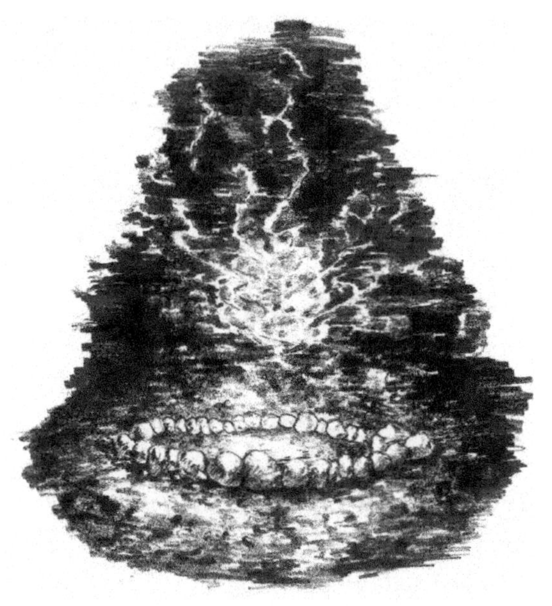

The Kuela continued to circle ahead of them, leading them to the western edge of the island. When they reached the beach, the bird flew out over the water. Joshua squinted but couldn't see anything obvious. There were no islands or any other features as far as the eye could see. The only thing visible was a jagged rock poking up out of the water. The Kuela circled above it and squealed. It flew directly above the rock, flapped its wings and landed atop it.

"What's that rock it landed on?" Joshua asked, turning to Luana.

"That can't be right," Luana said, looking confused.

"Why? What's wrong? What is it?" Joshua asked.

"That's…that's K'pia."

"K'pia?"

"Well, it's nothing more than a barren rock. You can only really see it fully at low tide. It marks the western boundary of Archipelago."

"Why has the Kuela brought us here?" Galleon asked. "Surely a flame can't exist if it's underwater half the time?"

"Well, exactly. That's what I don't understand."

"Have you ever been there?" Sarah asked.

"Well, no. I mean…there's really nothing to see. It's just a barren rock. It's underwater most of the time anyway."

"Can we take a look?" Joshua asked.

"Sure. I mean…I don't see why not, but there's really nothing to see. If we wait until low tide, we could probably walk out there. But I really don't think we'll find much when we get there. Maybe the Kuela got confused or something."

"How long before low tide?" Andrew asked.

"Oh, about an hour or so."

"Great. That gives us time to have something to eat," Andrew said.

"What, again?" Galleon scoffed. "You've only just finished stuffing your face with those Lili'kio things. Honestly, Andrew. Sometimes I think your stomach is a bottomless pit."

With an hour to kill, everyone sat around on the beach waiting for the tide to go out. Andrew and Galleon both gorged themselves with fruits. Before long, they were both snoring under the midday sun. By the time the tide was out, the rock revealed itself to be a roughly cone-shaped crag about three times Joshua's height. Ragged seaweed draped its sides.

"Luana, how long before the tide comes back in again?" Joshua asked.

"Not long, although I really don't think it's going to matter. There's nothing there to see, but there's certainly enough time to get there and back before the water starts to rise again."

Joshua looked at Andrew and Galleon, who were still snoring away.

"Sarah, maybe you'd better wait here and keep an eye on these two."

Sarah stepped closer to Joshua and took his hand. "You will be careful, Joshua, won't you?"

Joshua smiled. He raised his hand and moved a few strands of Sarah's hair to one side and she smiled back.

"We'd better get out there before the tide turns" Luana said, pointing to the rock.

"Come on, then," Joshua said to Luana. "Let's go and take a look while we still can."

Luana and Sarah glanced at each other as Joshua walked into the water. He turned and watched; their eye contact lingered longer than was comfortable.

Luana led Joshua across the ankle-deep shallows out to the rock, trying to dodge all the spiny urchins nestled into rock pools. The journey took about ten minutes. When they arrived, Joshua turned and waved back towards Sarah, who was still standing at the beach looking at them. She waved back and sat down.

Joshua and Luana made their way to the far side of the rock. When they got all the way around, Joshua noticed a small opening half submerged near the rock's base. It was just big enough to squeeze through. Joshua and Luana looked at each other with puzzled looks on their faces.

"I…I had no idea this…was here," Luana said, shaking her head and raising her eyebrows.

Joshua took a deep breath and exhaled. "Come on. Let's see what's inside."

"Ok, but we'll need to be quick. Once the tide starts coming in, it won't be long before this opening is submerged."

They exchanged nervous glances. Joshua got onto his knees and squeezed through the hole. Luana followed him in.

It was dark and they had to feel their way through the narrow fissure. Crawling on their knees through the water, they kept knocking themselves on the sharp edges of the tunnel wall.

They pushed through the cramped passageway for a couple of minutes before it opened out into a cavern big enough for them to stand. Right there in the centre of the cavern was a small blue flame. No bigger than a fist, it levitated above the ground at about waist height. A ring of rounded boulders encircled it. Water trickled down the inside of the cavern walls, onto which the blue flame cast eerie shadows.

"Wow," Luana said in awe, "could it be…the Flame of Eternity?" She took Joshua's hand and squeezed it tightly.

"It's okay," Joshua said softly. He gently clasped Luana's hand to reassure her. He waded around the flickering flame but there were no other features he could see other than the tunnel entrance. Joshua leant forward and squinted at the small fire.

Speaking softly, he gazed at it and said, "Are you…are you the Oracle?"

There was a pause. All at once the flame erupted and shot up into the air. The cavern above them seemed to extend to way beyond the height of the rock as it was visible from the outside. Both Joshua and Luana recoiled, shielding their eyes.

After a few moments, the flame died down again but was now much bigger than originally. Now it glowed a yellowish orange like the Oracle of Forestium. Small sparks emanated from the top of the flame. They floated up into the air trailing wisps of smoke.

Then a sweet voice echoed in the cave.

"The pure of heart may command the flame, for he is worthy that the Oracle may assist."

Each soft word spoken by the Oracle was accompanied by another spark flying into the air trailing a wisp of smoke.

Luana's eyes widened. "Are…are you the Flame of Eternity?" she asked.

"I am known as many things in many worlds."

More wisps of smoke trailed more sparks as the Oracle spoke.

"I…I need your help," Joshua said, leaning forward some more. "I need to open the Portallas…to free my people. Can you help?"

Joshua's jaw hung open in anticipation. There was a pause before the Oracle again spoke.

"Your people are not of this world, Joshua. Your destiny is a perilous one. The power He yields will not easily be vanquished. I can only reveal the truth. You must accept it willingly."

Joshua straightened up. He pondered the Oracle's words. *What truth was the Oracle referring to? What did she mean by "accept willingly"?* He leaned forward again.

"I…I'm ready to hear the truth."

His eyes widened further. He wasn't sure he wanted to hear what the Oracle was going to say next but he bit his lip, waiting with bated breath.

Without warning, there was a blinding flash. Joshua found himself completely engulfed within the flame, which was frozen all around him. He felt a dizzy sensation as he levitated above the ground. He could see Luana standing in the water, but she wasn't moving. She, too, was frozen in time.

The Oracle's sweet timbre sounded again. This time, instead of bouncing off the cave walls, the voice came from within his own mind, as if he was thinking the words directly.

"To free your people, you must bring the three orbs of this world together, Joshua. But beware, for the Orb of Sacrifice demands a life…one who cares for you deeply. The knowledge of this is the price you must pay."

Joshua's heart raced. The Oracle's words sent a wave of anguish through him.

"He that vanquished your people grows more vulnerable with each Portallas that you open. But heed this warning, Joshua, for a terror has been unleashed on my children. It is of the like not seen in this world before. I fear for my people here. A weapon forged from the fire that created this world can defeat the beast. I have kept it hidden for centuries. Only one that has killed can command it. You must hurry, Joshua, for the terror is close at hand."

The Oracle's voice faded into an echo. There was another blinding flash. When Joshua opened his eyes again, he was once more standing next to Luana in the cave, her hand clasped tightly to his. The orange fire shrunk until it was once again a small, fist-sized blue flame, flickering in the cavern.

"I…I don't get it," Luana said, shaking her head. "Wasn't the Flame of Eternity going to tell you the truth or something?"

Joshua turned to Luana with wide eyes.

"It did."

Luana shook her head in confusion.

"Um, never mind. Come on, let's get out of here. The water is rising."

Luana scanned the water's surface. The level was now at their knees. "You're right. Let's go. Quickly! Or we'll never get out of here."

As they turned to exit the cavern, Luana noticed something.

"Hold on! What's that? Was that there before?"

She pointed to a wrapped bundle of leaves floating on the surface of the water beneath the flame. Joshua reached down to pick it up. He tucked in into his keeper bag and said, "Come on, we need to get out of here while we still can."

Joshua followed Luana into the small tunnel and they both squeezed through the narrow passage. The water level rose quickly. As they crawled on all fours, they were barely able to breathe through the narrow passage of air between the water at their chest and low ceiling. Salt water lapped at their faces. Trying to control his breathing, Joshua gulped a mouthful of water. It sent him into a fit of coughing. By the time he could see light at the end of the tunnel, the water was up to his face. He had to turn his head sideways to keep his mouth out of the water. Taking a last lungful of air, he ducked under the water and swam the remaining section of the tunnel. At the end, he found Luana's hand reaching into the entrance of the tunnel. He grabbed it and she pulled him to the surface.

"Come on," Luana pleaded as he stood up to take in a fresh lungful of air. "We need to get back to shore quickly. These waters are infested with Mano'ana. We'll be lucky to make it back alive."

# CHAPTER SIXTEEN
## *The Dagger of Pa'hoa*

Joshua and Luana emerged from behind K'pia to see Sarah, Andrew and Galleon all standing on the shore and waving at them.

"Quickly, we must hurry," Luana screamed. "The waters will already be teeming with Mano'ana."

The current swirled back and forth around the rock with every wave. It pushed hard against their bodies, making it difficult to maintain their footing. As the two of them struggled to hasten their way back across the now waist-deep water, Joshua felt a sudden jolt of electricity and collapsed into the water. It was followed by another, sending searing pain shooting down the length of his body. Luana grabbed his arms, pulling him upright. Then, she, too, was struck. She muffled a gasp as she sank into the icy water. Still struggling to maintain his own footing, Joshua reached out, hoping to grab her.

Then, Joshua felt someone grab him. It was Andrew. Joshua's childhood friend lifted his numb arm over his shoulders and helped him towards the shore.

"Luana—" he tried to turn back but his legs wouldn't function.

"One at a time," Andrew panted.

Sarah rushed past them. Luana was struggling weakly, only her left hand trying to swim.

Sarah pushed her way through the water, lunging for Luana. Joshua looked over his shoulder, still unable to stand and crippled with searing agony. Sarah pulled Luana backward through the water. Through blurred vision, Joshua watched as Sarah's body jerked. Dark shadows circled the two girls, and Sarah toppled, still striving to drag Luana into the shallower water.

Andrew dropped Joshua onto the sand and ran back into the water.

Joshua felt the life fading from him. Barely able to breathe, he closed his eyes and everything faded into darkness.

Joshua opened his eyes beneath a blanket of blue sky. A face came into his field of view, shielding him from the glare of the sun. It was Sarah.

"Joshua? Are you all right?" her voice echoed.

"W…what happened?" Joshua pushed himself into a seated position on the sand.

Sarah flung her arms around Joshua's shoulders, smothering him with affection.

"Thank goodness you're safe," she said, kissing him, then cradling his face against her.

"You nearly died, that's what," Galleon said. "Those Mano'ana things really have taken a disliking to you."

Joshua held his hands in front of him and wiggled his fingers. "I…I can still feel the tingling."

"That'll pass in a few minutes," Luana said. "You were stunned about four or five times I think. You really are lucky to be alive, Joshua. If it wasn't for Andrew and Sarah here, we would both have been killed."

Joshua couldn't help but notice the sorrow in Luana's eyes as Sarah continued to fuss over him. Joshua wanted to say something to her but she turned away before he got the chance.

"Thanks, Andrew," Joshua said, turning to his best friend. Andrew held out an arm and helped Joshua to his feet. Sarah hugged him again. Joshua stared out towards K'pia, which was now almost submerged again. He saw numerous dark shadows in the water circling the rock, where dozens of Mano'ana still thrashed about below the waters surface.

"Well?" Galleon said, peering at Joshua with raised brows.

"Well what?" Joshua asked, looking bemused.

"What do you mean 'well what'? I'm not taking a bloody survey. What happened? Where did you disappear to?"

"The two of you were gone for ages," Sarah said, releasing Joshua from her embrace. "After you disappeared behind K'pia, the water started rising. We thought…well, we thought the worst."

"Did you find the Oracle?" Galleon asked, staring at Joshua. He leaned in with eyebrows raised.

Joshua and Luana exchanged glances. "Yes, we found it, all right."

"And?"

"It was like it was in Forestium. I…I spoke with the Oracle. Or rather, the Oracle spoke to me…sort of."

Joshua lowered his brow, trying to remember it all. He shifted his eyes as though trying to digest what had happened.

"What do you mean, sort of?" Galleon asked.

"Well…it's hard to explain. The Oracle said I had to bring the three orbs together—like Epani said when we were back on Ulaia."

"Is that it? You mean you barely escaped death just to be told something you already knew? Bloody hell, Joshua. I would have expected more from an Oracle."

"Well…there's more. The Oracle spoke about a terror—or something—that the Goat has unleashed. At least, I think it was unleashed by the Goat. It was all…sort of…confusing."

"Is that it?" Galleon asked, looking a tad disappointed.

"Let the man speak!" Andrew said, elbowing Galleon.

Joshua thought for a moment. Then he remembered what the Oracle had said about using the Orb of Sacrifice. She had said it demanded a sacrifice from someone that cared for him. Joshua caught Sarah's eye and a wave of dread washed over him.

"So, what's this terror, then?" Andrew asked.

"Hmm?" Joshua said, snatching himself back into the moment. "Oh, um, I don't know, but the Oracle gave me this."

Joshua reached into his keeper bag and pulled out the bundle of leaves.

"What's that?" Sarah asked.

"I don't know. The Oracle said this could be used to defeat the monster. Only—" Joshua concentrated, trying to remember Oracle's words. "Yes, that's it, it won't work unless someone that has killed before uses it. Yes, I think that's what she said."

"Well, open it up and see what it is!" Galleon said, shifting on his feet and now rubbing his hands together with an excited look in his eye.

Joshua carefully removed the leaves one by one. Inside was a dagger. About the length of Joshua's forearm, it had a shiny blade, serrated on one side. It was curved and narrowed to a sharp point. The handle was covered with shells. Joshua took it in his hand and held it up so they could get a good look. The smooth, shiny blade shimmered in the sunlight.

"So, this is what the Oracle gave you to fight whatever this thing is the Goat has unleashed?" Andrew asked, looking a little confused.

"Seems so," Joshua said, nodding.

"But hold on. Have you ever killed before?" Andrew asked. Joshua shook his head.

"Have any of us killed anyone before?" Andrew asked, turning to the others. "I know I haven't."

Everyone turned to each other and they all shook their heads.

"So…who's going to use it, then?"

They all stared back at the dagger.

"Luana, have you seen this before? Do you know anything about it?" Joshua asked.

Luana shook her head. "No, but we could take it to Tu'hutu. She might know more about it."

"Tu'hutu?" Joshua asked. "Who's that?"

"A really old and really wise woman, who also happens to be my grandmother. If anyone knows anything about this dagger, it would be her."

"Okay," Joshua said, stashing the dagger back into his keeper bag, "what are we waiting for? Let's get going."

"We can't. Not yet, at least. It's going to be dark soon and it's too dangerous. We'll have to go in the morning."

"Do we need to go to another island, Luana?" Sarah asked.

Luana glanced at Sarah and nodded. "Tu'hutu lives in Piya'ata. It's a village on Atoweena."

"Hold on. Which island?" Andrew asked, scratching the side of his head. "I'm losing track of it all."

"Atoweena, the island where Luana is from." Sarah said to Andrew. "You know, the one you first arrived on?"

"That's right," Luana said, nodding.

"Okay, so hold on," Galleon said, staring into space. He was tapping his chin and thinking hard. "So, we're on Kuela's Nest Island now," he said slowly and in a contemplative voice, "and we got here from Ulaia, and—"

"Atoweena will be visible again when we reach the other side of this island," Luana said, cutting Galleon off mid-thought. "You can get to Atoweena from all the islands we've been to so far. It's one of the biggest islands in Archipelago."

Galleon stopped, his jaw still hung open, and said, "Um, yeah. What she just said."

Just then, a small flock of Kuelas flew overhead. They were screeching.

"Hmm, that's strange," Luana, said, looking up at the agitated birds.

"What's strange about it?" Galleon asked. "I mean, we are on Kuela's Nest Island, right? If they were Raetheons, that'd be strange."

"It's…well they just seem a bit—"

Luana squinted at the birds as they disappeared over the treetops and out of sight. After a moment, she shook her head and said, "It's probably nothing. Come on, we can camp here for the night."

"I'll get the camp setup," Sarah said, and she strode off to find some Kea'hee nuts.

"I'll help," Luana said, following her.

With the light fading, Luana and Sarah had to walk some distance before Luana finally spotted some Kea'hee nuts.

Luana bent down to pick them up. Handing them to Sarah, she said, "You really do love him, don't you."

Sarah smiled. "He means everything to me." She sighed, reflecting back on everything that had happened since she first met Joshua. "We've been through a lot together in a short space of time." Then she smiled again, saying, "He makes me laugh. I couldn't imagine being without him now."

After a pause, Luana said, "I'm sorry, Sarah."

"Sorry? Why, have you done something wrong?"

"I mean…well, you are both from a very different place. I thought you weren't…you know. Well, I just didn't think the two of you were—"

"It's okay. I think I understand. We've found this place to be very different to Forestium. Lots of new things, different customs and everything. I can only imagine how we must seem to you."

Luana smiled. "Come on. Let's get back to camp and get this fire going."

The past couple of exhausting days had caught up to everyone with fatigue setting in. Joshua's thoughts turned to Kahu'niti. By the time the camp fire was going, everyone sat in quiet contemplation.

"He's still out there," Joshua said, breaking the silence. Everyone turned to him. "Kahu'niti, I mean."

There was a pause, as this realisation sank in.

"We need to take this seriously, Joshua. We should take turns keeping watch," Andrew insisted.

"I'll take the first watch," Joshua said, beginning to get to his feet. "You can—"

"No! You need the rest more than anyone, Joshua. Galleon and I had some sleep earlier. I'll take the first watch. Galleon can relieve me in a few hours." Galleon nodded at Andrew.

"Andrew's right," Galleon said. "You and the girls can get some rest. If something does happen, we've at least got this dagger thing."

Joshua reached into his keeper bag and pulled out the dagger, still wrapped in the bundle of leaves. He handed it to Andrew.

Joshua stood up and walked over to the row of leaf sleeping bags they had arranged higher up the beach. He got into the one on very end and made himself comfortable. Sarah and Luana followed him.

"I'll take this one," Luana said, quickly stepping into the sleeping bag next to Joshua. "Sleep well," she said, closing her two palm fronds together. Sarah slipped into her sleeping bag and was soon off to sleep.

Galleon took the first watch.

Christopher D. Morgan

# CHAPTER SEVENTEEN
## *The Ke'ahi Festival*

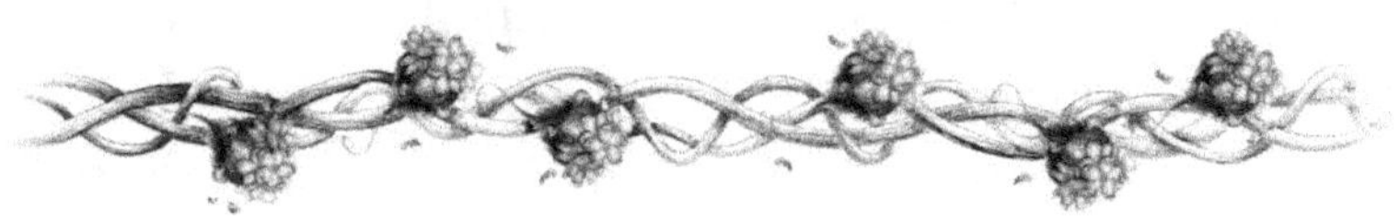

Joshua opened his eyes the next morning to find himself the last to awake. Everyone else had already begun their day. Luana was collecting berries and Sarah was shaking the sand out of the clothes she had hung to dry. Andrew was stuffing his face with berries by the fire and Galleon was busy trying to remove shells from between his toes.

"Did you sleep well?" Luana asked, walking up to Joshua and handing him a handful of berries.

"Hmm, yes, thanks. How long have you all been up?"

"Not long. What do you think of these? They only grow here."

"Hmm," Joshua nodded his approval. "That's really good."

"Here, let me try one of them." Sarah arrived and sat beside Joshua. She took one of the berries Joshua was holding and placed it into her mouth. "Hmm," she said. "These are delicious, aren't they?" She then put another one into Joshua's mouth and gave him a quick kiss.

Luana's smile faded as she watched. Once again, Joshua noticed that sadness in her eyes.

Joshua and Sarah caught each other's eye as Luana got to her feet and walked off.

"Did you see that?" Joshua asked Sarah, leaning in so his words wouldn't be overheard.

"Yeah. I spoke to her last night. She realise we're a couple now but I think she still idolises you. You're the one that the Oracle spoke to, remember? You're the one that's been entrusted with the Dagger of Pa'hoa. You're the one with the Orb of Sunshine. These are all things that are the stuff of legend in this world. In a funny way, you're probably the closest thing to a god she's ever encountered."

"I'm no god," Joshua dismissed.

"Sure, but just look at it from her perspective for a minute."

Joshua thought about the situation. He let out a deep sigh. "Okay, let's get going. I want to find out more about this dagger."

Luana kicked sand onto the fire.

"Right," Galleon said, having removed the last of the shells from his feet. "Where did you say we're heading to?"

"Atoweena," Luana replied. "One of the villages there is called Piya'ata."

"Right," Galleon said, scratching his head and nodding in Andrew's direction. "Got that Andrew? We're going to see someone called Tu'hutu in a place called Piya'ata on the island of Atoweena...or something. All clear?"

Andrew chuckled at his friend. "Don't worry. Your mental map of this place is bound to get better eventually."

They followed the northern beaches for about an hour before the main island of Atoweena came into view.

"You said Atoweena was the largest island here, Luana?" Andrew asked.

"It's actually not the biggest but certainly one of them. It is the most inhabited, though. There are quite a few villages there. The largest of the islands, Lua'pele, lies to the east of Atoweena. It's little more than a volcano and nobody lives there."

"So, how are we going to get back to Atoweena from here?" Andrew asked.

"If we go a little farther, there's a sandbank that will be visible at low tide. We can walk across it."

"Um, will there be any of those Mano'ana eels?" Joshua asked, coming to an abrupt halt. There was a slight tremor in his voice.

"No, don't worry," Luana said with a hint of a chuckle. "Besides, we'll be on Atoweena long before the tide rises again."

Sure enough, they traversed the sandbank and made it to Atoweena with no sign of any Mano'ana. As soon as they were safely on the other side, a Kuela flew over the treetops and circled above them. Luana held out her arm and the graceful bird glided over to it and landed. It cooed and nudged Luana's cheek.

"Won't we need to see the Protector first?" Sarah asked. "You said something earlier about needing to see the Protector whenever you visit an island."

Luana nodded. "Only those islands that have villages on them have a Protector, of course — like Atoweena does. We have to pass through Hulawei to get to Piya'ata first anyway, so we can stop in and see the Protector on the way."

The group travelled for another hour before seeing signs of human habitation. As they strolled into Hulawei, Joshua noticed a handful of Kuelas screeching overhead. Luana squinted at them. Joshua sensed something was amiss.

"What is it, Luana?" Joshua asked.

She slowly shook her head.

"I don't know. They aren't usually this agitated."

As they walked into Hulawei, Joshua noticed there was nobody about. The last time he was here, there were dozens of villagers but the village was now eerily empty.

Luana led them into the main building in the centre of the village. Inside, it was empty. Not a soul was to be found.

"That's strange," Luana said. "There's always *someone* here."

"Maybe they all went fishing?" Andrew suggested.

Luana shook her head.

"Well, maybe they are at one of the other villages?" Galleon asked.

Luana heaved a big sigh. "Something's not…I don't know. I just sense…come on, maybe someone at Piya'ata can explain."

Luana led them out of the building and back into the thick vegetation. A well-trodden path led them the hour journey all the way to Piya'ata. As they neared, Luana's pace quickened. Through the trees ahead, Joshua noticed flames. Fearing the worst, everyone ran to see what was happening.

The path led to a clearing. Luana stopped and everyone caught up with her.

Several dozen villagers stood in a circle in the middle of the clearing, clapping and cheering. Many were ornately decorated with costumes and coloured feathers in their hair, like Luana's. Flames were shooting above their heads. Joshua stood on tiptoes but couldn't see where the flames were coming from.

"Luana, what is it? What's going on?" Joshua asked.

Luana took a sharp intake of breath. She turned and beamed.

"No wonder the Kuelas were on edge. It's the Ke'ahi Festival. With everything that has happened over the past couple of days, I'd completely forgotten."

"The Ke'what festival?" Andrew asked, having caught up. He was panting and looking perplexed.

"Ke'ahi. It's a time to celebrate. Come!"

She led them all through the throng of villagers. A tall and muscular man with decorated arms and face danced in the centre of the action. He was moving in a circle around a fire pit, stomping on the ground to the rhythmic banging of drums. Several villagers dressed in flamboyant costumes sat on the far side of the circle, each banging on a drum in a rhythmic, alternating sequence. Between the drumming and chanting, the musical cacophony was loud but pleasing.

The decorated villager in the centre was spinning a wooden spear with balls of fire on either end. The roaring flames flew around his body as he performed a spectacular dance. The balls of light moved so fast, they created the effect of a continuous circle of flames around him. Other villagers all clapped and cheered in time to the drumming.

Joshua enjoyed the distraction. Before long, he and the others were clapping along to the music.

"What is this celebration?" Joshua asked, leaning closer to Luana so that she could hear him.

"It's a celebration of the sun. Tomorrow will be when the sun is at its highest point in the sky. We dance to give thanks for the sun providing us with warmth and protection. Come, shall we dance?"

"Dance?" Joshua said, looking quite uncomfortable. "I, um, I don't—"

"Here," Luana said to Sarah, turning her so that she faced away, "it's traditional for the women of Atoweena to wear their hair up."

Luana expertly tied Sarah's hair up into a bun and secured it with two colourful Kuela feathers.

"What do you think, Joshua?" Luana asked, showing off her handiwork with Sarah's hair.

The two girls now appeared very similar from behind. Joshua admired Sarah's beautiful new hairstyle. He raised his hand to her hair and stroked the colourful feathers in it. There was something about it—something he couldn't quite put his finger on.

Before Joshua could give it any more thought, Luana took him by the hand and pulled him into the centre of the circle. All the villagers cheered as Luana danced alongside the fire dancer with the flaming spear. Not knowing what he should do, Joshua shied away to the side. He tried to move his arms to the music, but ended up flailing them haphazardly in an uncoordinated fashion, feeling very self-conscious.

"Go on, Joshua!" Andrew shouted. "What are you waiting for? Shift those hips!" He and Galleon turned to each other laughing.

Shrugging his shoulders, Joshua joined in and did his best to match Luana's dance moves. Despite Joshua's obvious lack of coordination, everyone clapped and cheered.

"They make a lovely dance pair, don't you think?" Galleon shouted to Sarah. "You're not the jealous type, are you?"

"It's all good fun," Sarah answered, smiling. "Anyway, it'll be good for him to unwind a little. He's been under a lot of stress lately."

A couple more villagers came over and took Galleon by the arms. Despite his protests, they led him off to somewhere out of sight.

"Where are they taking him?" Sarah said to Andrew.

"No idea. Maybe they're cannibals?" Andrew replied, with a huge grin on his face.

Sarah pursed her lips and turned sharply to Andrew and said, "That's not —"

But before she had a chance to finish her sentence, a flamboyantly dressed villager with a huge plume of feathers on her head walked up and offered them both a small bowl. It was half filled with a brown, muddy liquid. The villager nodded and raised her brow. Andrew and Sarah glanced at each other sheepishly.

"Um, what's that?" Andrew asked.

The woman didn't reply but again pushed the cup towards him.

"Well? Go on," Sarah said, egging Andrew on. "You don't want to offend her, do you?" Sarah had a wry look of satisfaction on her face.

Andrew pulled a distinctly false grin, staring at the bowl. The woman stood before him, continuing to nod and smile. Andrew looked back and forth between Sarah and muddy liquid. Andrew shrugged his shoulders and took the bowl. He then tilted his head back and tipped its contents into his mouth. A split second later, he spat the whole lot out again, spraying nearby villagers. Sarah burst into laughter.

As Andrew burst into a fit of coughing, there was an eruption of cheering and laughter that rang out around the festival. Everyone pointed to the far side of the clearing. There, held aloft on the shoulders of two decorated villagers, was Galleon. He had a messy plume of feathers on his head and his face was painted like one of the drummers.

"I told you to *put me down*. Honestly!"

It was no use. Galleon's protestations were ignored and he was carried aloft like a ceremonial statue, much to everyone else's amusement. Sarah and Andrew doubled over with laughter. Sarah then ran into the middle of the circle, dancing along with Joshua and Luana.

# CHAPTER EIGHTEEN
## *Tu'hutu*

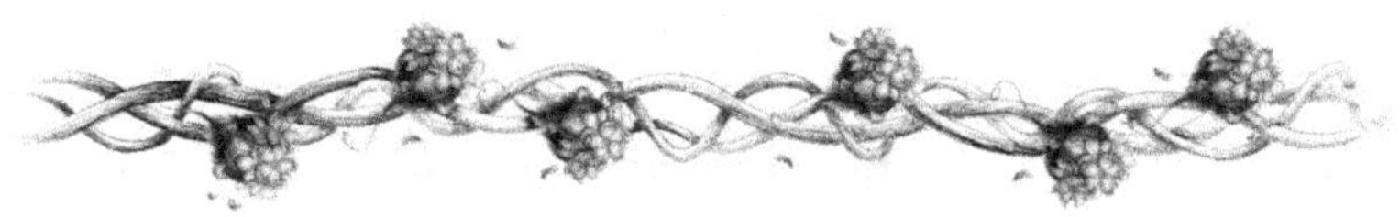

The Ke'ahi festival continued into the night. As outsiders, Joshua and the others received a lot of attention and they thoroughly enjoyed themselves. Even Galleon found himself having fun after a while, being carried around like a king.

With the merriment looking like it wasn't going to stop any time soon, Joshua and the others found a quiet spot on the edge of the clearing to catch their breaths and watch the continued celebrations.

"Have you tried that drink they've been handing out?" Andrew asked Galleon.

"Yeah. It's disgusting. I've tasted three-week-old Wood-boar piss better than that. I nearly threw up after trying it and now half my tongue is numbed."

"Galleon! Watch your language!" Sarah said, casting him a scathing look.

"What? What did I say?" He said, feigning innocence.

A frail old lady leaning on a bamboo cane emerged from one of the huts on the perimeter of the clearing. A short woman, she was wearing a long dress. It was brightly decorated with colourful feathers and native flowers. She had her hair up in a tight bun with small pieces of bamboo poking through it. Skin hung from her wrinkly old face. Despite her short stature, she was quite imposing. Each time a villager passed her, they stopped and bowed.

"Who's that woman over there?" Joshua asked

"Someone of importance by the looks of things. Maybe the Protector's mother?" Sarah suggested.

"Protector's great grandmother more like it. Whoever it is, she looks ancient. Look at the old dear. She's on her last legs, bless her."

"Galleon, really!" Sarah said, this time turning to him with her hands on her hips.

"What did I say?" Galleon replied with a shrug, doing his best to pretend he was unaware of having said anything inappropriate. Andrew didn't quite manage to stifle a snigger, much to Sarah's disdain.

The old woman scanned the area until she spotted Joshua and the others. She peered in his direction and squinted. Just at that moment, Luana walked up to her. They exchanged a few words and then the old woman turned and went back inside. Luana waved across the clearing to Joshua, beckoning him and the others over. They made their way over to where Luana was standing.

"Come," Luana said, "I want you to meet Tu'hutu." She then led them in.

Through the doorway, there was a small passage that led to a curtain of reeds. Luana pushed her way in and held the curtain open with one hand so the others could follow. The round hut was well lit by a fire in the centre. Smoke rose up from the dancing flames and out through a hole in the top of the thatched ceiling.

Joshua peered around. Hanging on the walls around the edge of the hut's interior were elaborately decorated tapestries. They were draped from the ceiling all the way to the floor and covered almost all of the wall space. Each featured a painting of an island.

"Come! Sit!" came a curt voice from the other side of the fire. The old woman was sitting there on the floor with her legs crossed. She looked like a red tent with a head poking through the top. Her expression portrayed a lack of patience. Everyone looked for somewhere to sit.

Joshua took a seat on the opposite side of the fire to her. Andrew and Sarah found positions either side of him. Luana took a seat next to her grandmother. This left little space for Galleon to sit. The only remaining spot was adjacent to the old woman. Everyone waited patiently for Galleon, the last to be seated. He pondered where he was going to sit. It created an awkward silence with everyone wondering what he was going to do next.

"Um…right," he said, bouncing on his toes and looking sheepish. "I'll…um. I'll sit here then. Next to, um, great grandma."

Andrew closed his eyes and put his palm to his face. He then peered through his fingers, shaking his head. Sarah gave Galleon her most scolding look yet. Galleon returned a look of dismissive bemusement.

"What's your name, boy?" The old woman said, staring at Galleon.

"I'm not a boy!" Galleon retorted. "I'm a man, if you must know. My name is Galleon. Galleon the Great."

"Hmmm," she said, eyeing him up and down. "I've caught Opa'nu with bait bigger than you."

Galleon lowered his brow and glared at the woman, finally taking his place on the floor.

Andrew sniggered. The old woman shot him a stare and he wiped the smirk from his face.

"Tu'hutu," Luana said, breaking the tension, "these are the strangers who arrived here not long ago. They're my friends."

The old woman took her time looking at Joshua, Andrew and Sarah in turn. She scowled at Galleon and said, "Even him?"

Galleon opened his mouth to speak but the Tu'hutu cut him off.

"So, Luana, tell me about this dagger, then."

Luana nodded at Joshua. He reached into his keeper bag and removed the bundle of leaves. He passed it to Luana. Carefully unwrapping it, she removed the dagger and offered its handle to Tu'hutu. The old woman took one look at the dagger and said, "That's the Dagger of Pa'hoa. Where did you find it?"

"Dagger of P'what?" Andrew asked.

All eyes turned to Andrew. Tu'hutu glared at him, as if to scold him for speaking out of turn, but said nothing.

"Oh, um, sorry. I'll, um, just—"

Tu'hutu turned back to the dagger. She ran her finger along the length of the blade, turning it over in the light of the fire. She took in a deep breath and then sighed.

"The sacred texts tell of the story of the dagger. It is said to have great powers."

"What sort of power?" Galleon asked.

Tu'hutu turned to him and eyed him up and down slowly. "*Great* powers. Of course, you'll know all about that, being Galleon *the Great*."

Once again, Andrew sniggered and once again he removed the smile after everyone stared at him.

"The Dagger was forged from the volcano of Lua'pele," Tu'hutu continued, "when Archipelago first came into being. When the Orb of Sunshine first came down from the heavens to create the islands, the volcano erupted. A piece of molten lava flew high into the heavens and was caught in the beam of light that emanated from the orb. It is said that the power of the orb infused into the rock and caused it to form into the dagger."

"How long ago was this?" Joshua asked quietly, as Tu'hutu passed the dagger back to him.

"Long before our people inhabited these islands."

There was a long pause. The old woman took a deep sigh and said, "There's one more thing."

Everyone hung off her words. The flames from the fire shimmered against the smooth blade of the dagger.

"It is also written…that whoever possesses the Dagger of Pa'hoa…will meet with great destruction."

Suddenly, there was an ear-piercing scream, followed by cries of panic.

Christopher D. Morgan

# CHAPTER NINETEEN
## *Fury Unleashed*

Everyone except Tu'hutu leapt to their feet and ran out to see what was happening. There was utter pandemonium, with people screaming and running in all directions.

At the edge of the clearing were pairs of bright lights. Clicking sounds came from all directions. The lights moved into the centre of the clearing.

"PALM CRABS!" Luana screamed.

About a dozen enormous creatures were marauding through the village. Some had already latched on to villagers. Two villagers were on the ground by the fire pit in the centre of the clearing, each with a severed limb. One of them — a child — wasn't moving. The other was on his back screaming as an attacking beast, itself dripping with blood, crawled onto his chest and thrust one of its enormous pincers deep into the screaming man's throat. He fell silent.

Another villager was clawing at the ground, trying to drag himself away from a crab that had his ankle in a vice-like grip. As he screamed for help, two other villagers tugged at his arms, trying to free him from the attacking monster. The beast raised its free arm high into the air as if to gloat. The chilling sound of its pincers snapping open and shut rang out loudly. It then raised the other claw, still attached to the villager's leg, into the air. Held between the vicious animal's one claw and the two villagers trying to tug him free, the hysterical villager was suspended off the ground. There was a loud crunch as two pincers thrust together, slicing clean through the man's leg. He fell to the ground screaming, his severed foot still held by the animal. Blood oozed from the man's footless limb.

All around, villagers were hurling spears, pots and even burning logs from the fire at the hideous creatures but nothing they did made a difference.

Joshua watched in horror as one of the creatures scurried towards them.

"RUN!" Joshua screamed as loud as he could. Everyone else bolted into the forest. They managed to flee just as the beasts closed in, preventing Joshua's own escape. The young Woodsman stood, paralysed, as the dark creatures approached. Gripped by panic, Joshua stumbled backwards, falling to the ground. The bloodthirsty crabs were almost upon him when he held out his hand to try to defend himself. In it was the Dagger of Pa'hoa.

Without thinking, Joshua thrust the dagger right into the face of one of the animals. It let out a high-pitched shrieking noise and began vibrating. Cracks appeared around its exoskeletal joints. Light emanated from each crack as the crab's body was forced out through the disintegrating shell. It was like molten lava oozing from the beast. Its shell expanded, cracking at the seams. The dark creature vibrated violently until its shell blew apart. The explosion sent broken shards of shell at high speed in all directions.

Joshua clambered to his feet. He looked in disbelief at the dagger in his hand. More screaming came from the other side of the clearing. Two more crabs were thrashing their razor-sharp pincers towards a group of trapped villagers trying to fend them off with spears and flaming torches. The men were cornered between two huts with no way to escape. Joshua ran across the clearing and thrust the dagger into the back of one of the beasts. Within seconds, it exploded. The other crab turned its attention to Joshua. It was enough of a distraction to allow the trapped villagers a chance to escape. The beast before him raised its arms high into the air, snapping its claw open and shut.

Then, a high-pitched screech came from outside the village. It echoed right over them. It was so loud, Joshua had to hold his hands to his ears. All the Palm Crabs crouched to the ground, creeping backwards towards the outer edge of the clearing. They all raised their claws, creating a cacophony of clacking. Their eyes lit up. Shards of light illuminated the clearing in pairs of brilliant, white beams of light. The rays scanned back and forth across the clearing.

There was a rumbling sound. The ground trembled like an earthquake, shaking the surrounding trees.

Joshua looked up to see something appearing over the top of the palms. Two enormous beams of light shone down into the clearing. They were so bright they lit up the village like daylight. Trees came crashing to the ground as an enormous monster came bursting through into the clearing. It was twenty times bigger than any Palm Crab Joshua had seen before.

Dozens of crabs, their eye beams criss-crossing the clearing, scurried between its legs. The huge beast waved one of its arms, which sent crabs scuttling in various directions. The monster's claw swept to one side, tearing through huts and trees like they weren't even there. It left swathes of empty space in its wake, strewn with village debris.

Joshua stood there, the dagger held out in front of him. Crabs approached him from all directions. The wide beams of the enormous beast's eyes swept back and forth across the clearing before locating Joshua. The light blinded him. More vicious creatures advanced towards his position. He tried to find an escape route but there were too many of them.

The giant Palm Crab raised its claw. All the smaller animals followed suit. Joshua gripped the dagger tightly, thrashing it back and forth in front of him. The animals continued their relentless advance. There was no way he would survive. He had to make a break for it. Joshua spun around. There was a small gap between two animals. He ran through it, narrowly dodging the crab's claws, and sprinted into the vegetation, his legs taking him as fast as he could run. The continued cacophony from behind him faded but he kept on running, faster and faster.

Joshua had no idea how long he had been running when an opening in the trees appeared before him and he leapt for it. He found himself sprinting out onto a beach and down to the water's edge. Light from the full moon shimmered across the still waters, punctuated by specks of starlight from the cloudless night sky.

The young Woodsman turned to look at the forest. Still gripped by panic, he panted heavily, sweat pouring from his face. If his heart were a cannon, it would have shot right through his chest.

He stood there, momentarily stunned, and watched the tree-line intently — hoping — begging nothing would emerge.

Christopher D. Morgan

# CHAPTER TWENTY

## *After the Attack*

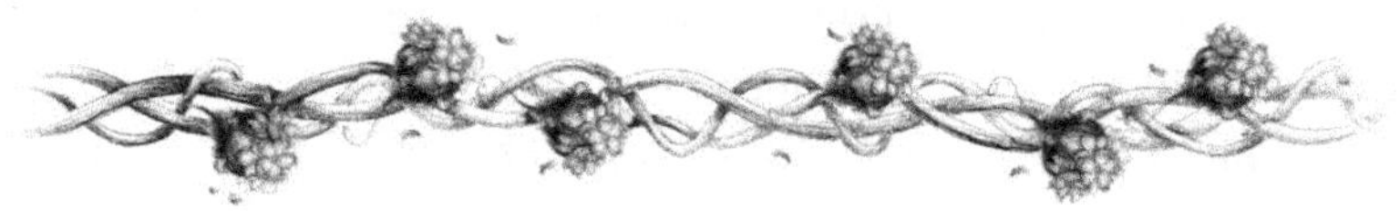

After a while, Joshua's heavy panting subsided and his heartbeat slowly calmed down. Seconds turned into minutes. There were no lights, no sounds, nothing. Now it was pitch black, and with the cold setting in, he was not even sure where he was or which direction he had run. With the panic of the attack abating, he became more aware of his surroundings. He was sweating, exhausted, afraid and alone.

Joshua scanned up and down the featureless beach. It stretched on into the distance in both directions with no landmarks to indicate where he was. With no moon, he couldn't see far under the twinkling starlight of the night sky. It was a calm night with very little cloud cover. The waves broke gently over the sandy beach. The rhythmic sound might otherwise have been soothing but Joshua's veins still pulsed with fear from the attack.

Choosing a direction he believed would lead him farther away from the village he had just fled, he set off.

The cool night air was chilling. Joshua rubbed his upper arms with both hands to try to generate some warmth. He had no idea how long he had been walking before he noticed something. Just ahead and barely visible were some markings on the sand. As he neared, he saw they were footprints. Joshua ran up and studied them closely. The lack of light made it difficult to see but they appeared to be freshly formed.

Joshua tracked the prints under the dim starlight. They came from the tree line and led off into the distance in the same direction he was already walking, so he decided to follow them.

After about a half hour of tracking, Joshua saw a small, flickering light in the distance. Erring on the side of caution, he crept close to the tree line to avoid being spotted. As he got closer to the light, crouching low and moving with stealth, he could see a figure sitting near the fire. It was little more than a silhouette and not at all clear if it was a man or woman. Joshua's heart skipped a beat as the thought struck him it might be Kahu'niti.

A shivering Woodsman from another world, Joshua felt alien and out of place here. His anxiety once again starting to soar, he crept still closer. He tried as best he could not to make any sound, watching where he placed his feet. By now his heart was pounding in his chest as much as it did back at the village. He reached into his keeper bag and slowly pulled the Dagger of Pa'hoa from it. The figure in front of the fire stood up and looked his way. Joshua froze, holding his breath, the dagger held out in front of him. After a few seconds, the figure turned, then crouched down again. Joshua carefully raised his head. He slowly straightened his legs to stand up.

Suddenly, a hand tapped Joshua on his shoulder. He spun around and thrust the dagger out in front of him.

"Joshua!" Andrew said, taking a quick step back, his hands raised in surrender.

"Andrew? You scared the living daylights out of me. I could have killed you."

"It's okay, it's just me. Galleon said he thought he saw something in the distance so I doubled back to see who it was. I was worried it might have been that madman."

"Kahu'niti? Yeah, I thought that's who it was by the fire."

Joshua heaved a big sigh. He stowed the dagger back into his keeper bag.

"What happened to you?" Andrew asked. "After we ran out of the village, we heard rumbling. We thought it was an earthquake or a volcano erupting or something. When we all caught up with each other, we couldn't find you so we feared the worst"

"Where is everyone else? Did everyone escape? Are they all safe?"

"Yeah, we're all fine. Luana and Galleon are collecting berries. That's Sarah by the fire up there. Come on. They'll all be pleased to see you're safe and sound."

Joshua and Andrew walked towards the fire. Sarah spun around when she heard them approaching.

"Joshua? Is that you?"

Seeing Andrew and Joshua come into the light of the fire, Sarah ran up to Joshua and flung her arms around him, hugging her boyfriend tightly.

"Here you go," Andrew said to Sarah. "I found something you lost."

"Thank goodness you're safe," Sarah said, showering Joshua with kisses. "We feared the worst. We've been looking for you everywhere for hours."

Galleon and Luana emerged from the tree line and walked up to the fire. They each dropped an armful of berries onto a leaf that was lying next to it. Luana beamed at the sight of Joshua.

"Well, I'm…just glad…you're all…safe," Joshua said, trying to get the words out whilst being kissed.

Luana watched Sarah, her smile fading.

"Where the hell have you been, then?" Galleon asked. "We thought you'd been eaten alive by those bloody Palm Crabs."

Luana threw a few dried palm frond tufts onto the fire. It erupted into a roaring flame. Three Opa'nu wrapped in leaf strips were leaned against the fire, steam rising from them.

"Yeah, I very nearly was," Joshua said. He stepped closer to the fire to warm his hands over it. "You won't believe what happened. Those Palm Crabs? I managed to kill two of them."

"You killed two Palm Crabs?" Luana said with stunned amazement. "How did you manage that? It's almost impossible to kill one of those things."

"It was the Dagger of Pa'hoa. They just…exploded after I stabbed them with it. I can't explain it. But that's not all. Those beasts are nothing compared to the monster that showed up after you all left."

"Monster?" Galleon asked.

"Yeah. Massive. Like a Palm Crab only much bigger. It knocked over trees and buildings like they were twigs. The ground shook as it moved."

"What happened?" Luana said, a hint of nervousness in her voice. "Did you see… I mean, do you know what happened…to Tu'hutu?"

Joshua thought for a moment.

"I don't know. It was hard to tell. That thing knocked over some of the huts but I don't know what happened after I escaped."

Luana had a blank expression. Her eyes were puffy.

"She's old. She wouldn't have been able to run," she said in a timid voice. "We could go back? We could…try to…find her. Maybe we can…" Luana's voice trailed away, grief overcoming her. Joshua caught everyone's eye. He knew—even Luana did—going back was simply not an option.

Sarah got up and sat beside Luana. She put her arm around her shoulder and cradled Luana's head.

Everyone fell silent. Luana sobbed in Sarah's arms. Sarah rocked her gently.

"Look," Joshua said gently. "We don't know what happened after we left, Luana. Maybe the Palm Crabs left after that. Maybe they…"

Joshua lowered his head. Although he wanted to comfort Luana, deep down he knew—they all did—it was unlikely anyone survived the attack.

After a while, Luana fell silent and sat there staring into the dancing flames, still cradled by Sarah, the pair of them rocking gently back and forth. As the Opa'nu sizzled, the crackling fire punctuated the noise of the gently crashing waves.

"Well," Galleon said after a few minutes of sombre reflection. "There's little we can do for now. Let's, um…let's all have a bite to eat. No use worrying on an empty stomach."

Galleon and Andrew removed the Opa'nu from the fire and passed them out. Everyone picked at their food. An uncomfortable silence befell the group.

Joshua's mind raced with the thoughts of the terror he had witnessed today. He was no closer to finding the third orb and their situation had become catastrophically worse. No longer was it just a matter of opening the Portallas and finding a way home; now all the inhabitants of Archipelago were in mortal danger and Joshua felt it was all because of him: had he not come here, none of this would have happened.

With these disturbing thoughts plaguing him, Joshua found it difficult to sleep. Eventually, exhaustion overtook him, and he drifted off into an uneasy slumber.

# CHAPTER TWENTY-ONE
## *A friend Returns*

Joshua opened his eyelids. The first rays of dawn light stretched across the calm water before him. Sitting up, he rubbed his eyes and peered around. Galleon was crouched by the fire trying to re-ignite it with a fresh Kea'hee nut. Sarah was examining some new berries she had found but Luana's sleeping bag was empty.

Joshua got up and stretched with a big yawn.

"Morning," Galleon said. There was a loud crack as the Kea'hee nut burst into flames. The tufts of dried tinder he had arranged in a cone shape erupted, bringing the fire back to life.

"Bloody amazing thing, these nuts," Galleon remarked.

"Yeah, I wish we had them in Forestium," Andrew said, arriving back at the camp and going to warm his hands above the fire. "Can you imagine how much easier life would be if we had these?"

"I know, right? And what about these palm trees? Is there anything they can't do?"

"They can't bring people back to life," Luana said, emerging from the tree line with an armful of red berries. She made no eye contact but threw the berries down onto the sand by the fire. She remained there, expressionless.

Andrew and Galleon both looked at each other, unsure of what to say. Galleon opened his mouth and was about to speak. He stopped short and lowered his head.

"Luana…look, we really don't know what happened for sure," Joshua said. "For all we know, Tu'hutu escaped or…or maybe the Palm Crabs could have gone back to where they came from or something. We…we don't know."

"No…we do know," Luana said in a quiet voice, staring at the flame. "Nobody survived. They're all gone. The entire village. Everyone…gone."

"How do you know?" Joshua asked quietly.

Luana stared at him vacantly for a moment before turning back to the fire. "The Kuelas." She spoke in a sullen voice. "They tell me things. It isn't always easy to understand what they're thinking, but in this case…"

Joshua's shoulders sank and he lowered his head.

"It's all my fault. I should never have come here."

"You can't go blaming yourself, Joshua," Andrew said.

"He's right," Galleon said, standing up straight. "It was the Goat who kidnapped the people of Morelle to begin with. You had to do something and you did. I would have done the same and so would anyone else. The Oracle told you it was the Goat who sent that monster to kill you last night."

Joshua's thoughts turned to what the Oracle had told him. She said that a terror had been unleashed and that she feared for her people here. *What possible chance could anyone have against something that even the Oracle herself feared would be unstoppable?*

Joshua looked at Luana. She got to her feet and walked down the beach. She was looking out over the ocean, squinting. Joshua walked up beside her and followed her gaze. A Kuela was flying towards them from out over the waters. Luana tilted her head.

"That's odd," she said.

"What's odd?"

"There's no island out there. Where is it coming from?"

Everyone followed the Kuela as it flew closer and closer. Instead of flying high, as they normally did, this one hugged the surface of the water. The colourful bird flew right up to them, flapped its wings rapidly, fixing its position in the air ahead of them. It swooped in and landed right at the water's edge. The bird stood there for a moment, watching them. Then it began to change shape. It grew taller and its feathers receded. After a few seconds, it had morphed into the figure of a man.

"Epani!" Joshua exclaimed, his eyes wide.

Epani walked up to Luana and put one hand on her shoulder.

"I am sorry about what happened at the village, Luana. There was nothing anyone could have done. You are all lucky to have escaped with your lives. Had you not fled, the destruction from the beast would have been complete and we would not be standing here."

"Epani, what happened?" Joshua asked. "What was that thing? Where did it come from?"

"A horrific dark beast of the underworld. It knows only destruction and death. It is known as Hewa'luki."

"Back at the cave, you said the Goat has awakened an unstoppable beast. Is that it? Is that what attacked us last night?"

Epani nodded.

"The Goat knows you have two of the three orbs from this world. He will stop at nothing to prevent you from finding the third. He has sent someone to kill you. He very nearly did."

Joshua stared at Epani.

"Wait! It was you? The Kuela...back on the beach when Kahu'niti tried to attack me."

Epani smiled.

"But I don't even know where to find the third orb," Joshua said, holding his forehead in his palm. He felt downtrodden—dejected.

"You have already found it. But getting it will not be easy."

Joshua gave Epani a blank stare. "What do you mean?"

"The beast that attacked the village last night guards the orb."

"Guards it? How?"

"I have discovered that the orb resides within it. The beast will need to be destroyed if you are to get to the orb."

Joshua shook his head and paced back and forth. He bit his nails as he thought hard.

"The Oracle gave me the dagger. But...it's going to be impossible for me to get anywhere near that thing. Besides, even if I could, the Oracle said that only someone that had killed could use the dagger anyway."

"The dagger is the only thing that can stop Hewa'luki. If you do not stop it, Joshua—"

Epani paused. He caught Luana's eye.

"What will happen if it's not stopped?" Luana asked, fresh tears now running down her face.

Epani heaved a big sigh and said, "It is a mindless beast. It will not stop...until it has destroyed every last man, woman and child here in Archipelago."

Sarah gasped, her hand shooting to her mouth as Joshua's shoulders sank with the pit in his stomach.

"But…I've never killed anyone. None of us have, so what use is the dagger?"

Epani said nothing. Joshua clasped his face with both hands and took in a deep breath. With a slow exhale, he pulled his fingers down his cheeks and rested his chin on his fists. Joshua was conscious that all eyes were on him. He noticed the look on Luana's face. The sadness in her eyes was all too familiar. He had seen it before in the face of his own mother the day he left his home town. Joshua felt the weight of the whole world on his shoulders.

"Where is Hewa'luki now?" he asked Epani.

"I don't know. But it will be on the move. It is a relentless creature and will continue hunting for you for as long as it has the strength to do so."

"Please, Joshua," Luana pleaded. "You have to do something. You're the one the Flame of Eternity chose. You're the one with the power of the Dagger of Pa'hoa and the Orb of Sunshine. I know you can do it, I know it. Please, don't let my people suffer."

Joshua walked up to Luana. He lifted her chin and stared into her eyes. "Hey. I'll do everything I can, do you understand me?"

Luana nodded, barely able to manage a faint smile.

Andrew was looking perplexed.

"What is it?" Joshua asked, turning to his friend.

"The Orb of Sunshine," he said, his eyes lighting up. "Don't you remember? Back at the cave with Kahu'niti. It lit up when that Palm Crab attacked and it stunned it or something. Maybe it'll do the same to this Hewa…whatsitsname thingy."

"He's right," Galleon said. "If we can get close enough and activate the orb, it might stun it."

"And then what?" Joshua asked, shrugging his shoulders. "Even if it were possible and we got close enough. Who's going to use the dagger to kill it?"

"I may not be able to kill it, Joshua," Epani said, "however I may be able to help all the same. I can try to locate Hewa'luki for you."

"That's a good start. We'll try to come up with a plan in the meantime," Joshua said.

Epani stepped back towards the lapping water and started shrinking. He morphed once again back into the form of a beautiful Kuela and took to the air. The bird circled above their heads before heading inland and disappearing over the palm forest.

# CHAPTER TWENTY-TWO
## *More Dark Forces*

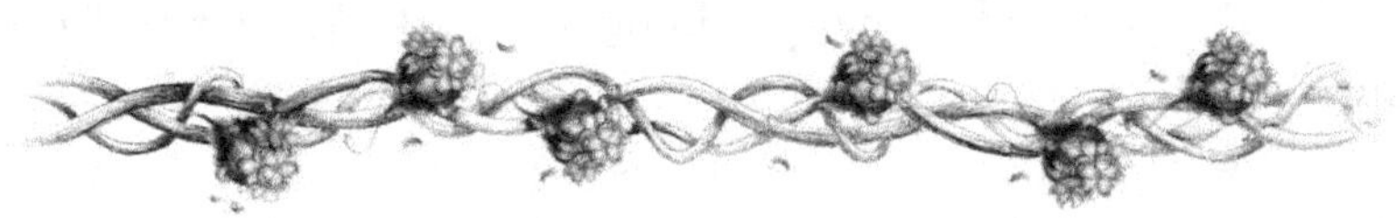

The Goat paced back and forth in His dark lair. The clicking from His hooves reverberated in the chamber. A damp mist hung in the stale air. What little light there was revealed the Goat's dark, contorted face. Two ribbed horns grew from the sides of His head, curling forward. A thick tuft of hair hung from his chin. The malicious creature mumbled to Himself. His tone was angry. He spoke slowly and with a deep loathing.

"Once again the boy has evaded my forces. Enough is enough! He must be stopped. If he opens another Portallas...I cannot allow—"

The Goat snorted, shaking his head violently. He stopped pacing. The chamber fell silent. With narrowed eyes, he stroked the tuft of untidy hair hanging from his chin.

"I must kill him quickly before I am weakened further. I must locate the boy."

His eyes shifted back and forth. He raised His head and peered up into a vaulted, dark space above him and howled. The noise echoed up into the empty chamber. Moments later, there was a clicking sound in the distance. Quiet to begin with, it approached from the void surrounding him in all directions. The sounds grew louder. They closed in on the Goat's location inside the chamber, intensifying. Soon, the entire space echoed with the sound of approaching Palm Crabs. Several pairs of lights came into view. One by one, the thorny beasts crawled out of the darkness. The dark creatures of the underworld raised their claws into the air, scurrying into a circle around the half-man, half-beast.

The Goat raised his one remaining hand. All the animals froze, plunging the dark chamber into an eerie silence. He waved to one side. One by one, each of the hideous crustaceans began to shrink, changing form. Their spiny outer shells sprouted black feathers. Within seconds, each of the horrific creatures had morphed into a scrawny bird. They were now all Kuelas. Like ordinary Kuelas but with none of the coloured feathers—just jet black all over, with a long, grey beak. Their feathers were scraggy, torn and untidy. The birds cackled and pecked violently at each other as they scampered across the floor.

"Go…find him!"

The black Kuelas flapped their wings and took to the air. They flew high up into the dark, vaulted ceiling space. After a few seconds, the flapping sound died. They were gone.

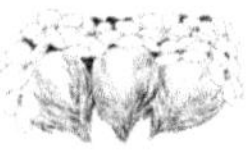

"Right," Joshua said with renewed determination. "We need a plan. If Epani does come back to us with the location of Hewa'luki, we're going to need to be ready."

Luana, who had been staring pensively out to sea, turned and said in a resounding tone, "I'm coming with you."

Joshua turned to her with a puzzled expression.

"Um…you're…coming with us?"

"Back to Forestium. If you do manage to open this Portallas thing, I want to come back with you to your world."

There was a moment of stunned silence as Joshua and the others took in what Luana had just said.

"There's nothing for me here now. All the people I love have been killed."

"But Luana—" Sarah started.

"My mind is made up," Luana said, cutting Sarah off dismissively. "Don't you understand? They're gone. They're all gone," she cried. "There's nobody left now."

There was a mixture of anger and despair in her tone. It was the first time Joshua had heard her express so much emotion. He walked over and put his arm around her shoulder. Luana cupped her face in her hands as she broke into tears. Joshua pulled her towards him and wrapped his arms around her. One by one, the others joined them.

Joshua felt his own eyes welling up. The sense of guilt he had been feeling was now more intense than ever. None of this would have happened if he hadn't come here to Archipelago.

Stepping back, Sarah said, "I'll, um…I'll go and see if I can find some berries or something."

"I'll go with you," Galleon suggested.

Sarah and Galleon walked off towards the palm trees and were soon out of sight.

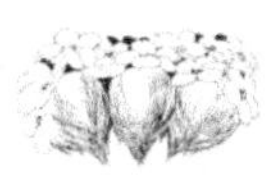

Sarah and Galleon rummaged around until they stumbled into a strange looking bush. The shrub was no taller than Galleon. About a dozen long, brown stems, no wider than a finger, all sprouted out from the centre. Each one arched outwards, creating a symmetrical pattern. At the end of each stem hung a thick bunch of leaves. Each bunch was weighed down towards the ground by a tightly packed cluster of bright yellow fruits. Sarah picked one of the fruits and peeled it open to see what it tasted like.

"Wow, these are amazing. Let's grab some," she said, handing one to Galleon for him to try.

"Hmm, lovely. I'm sure they'll do wonders for speeding things through my intestines."

Sarah let out a nervous chuckle. "I wonder how you tell which are the ripest? Luana said that the other fruits were the ripest when they had turned red but these are all a different colour. Do you think they're safe to eat? We should take some back with us. Maybe Luana can tell if they're safe to eat or not."

Galleon immediately spit out the piece he was chewing on.

Sarah chuckled, feeling each fruit in turn.

After a moment's pause, Galleon stepped closer to Sarah. "He still loves you, you know."

Sarah stopped what she was doing and sighed.

"Aren't you worried about Joshua?" Galleon asked.

She shook her head. "I'm more worried about Luana. She's under a lot of strain. That poor girl. I mean, just look at what's happened to her people. I can only imagine what she must be going through."

"Yeah, I know." Galleon lowered his head, speaking in a sullen tone. "I know what she's going through." He shook his head and sighed. "Losing your people...it's—"

Suddenly, a rasping noise echoed from overhead. Sarah and Galleon looked up. Through the gaps in the palm tree canopy they could see a jet-black Kuela flying over them. It screeched again, high-pitched and shrill. It was an unpleasant sound, not at all like the beautiful song they were used to from the colourful Kuelas.

They watched as the scrawny looking bird flew right over them before disappearing.

"That's not right," Sarah said slowly.

"I agree," Galleon said, still looking up. "Come on, let's get these fruits and find the others."

Collecting as many as they could hold, they made their way back towards the sea.

# CHAPTER TWENTY-THREE

## *Searching for the Beast*

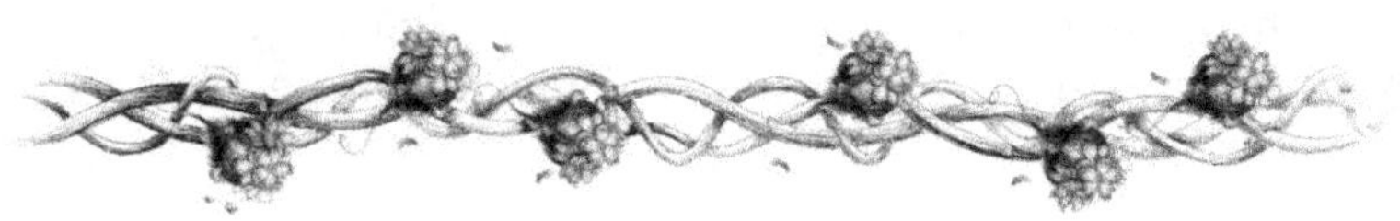

Before they reached the edge of the palm forest, Sarah and Galleon ran into the others.

"What's the matter?" Galleon asked as they met up, "where are you all going?"

"We had to run," Joshua said, panting. "There was this strange bird—"

"A black Kuela with a screech worse than Andrew's snore?" Galleon said. "Yeah, we saw it, too."

"What kind of Kuela was that, Luana?" Sarah asked.

"I…I don't know. I've never seen anything like it before."

"Maybe it's a scout," Andrew said.

Everyone turned to look at him.

"A scout?" Joshua asked.

"You know, like the Blood-bats in Forestium. Maybe it's something the Goat sent to try to find you."

Joshua stared pensively into the forest, running his fingers over his lips in deep thought.

"We'll have to remain out of sight from now on," Andrew declared. "We can't risk the Goat finding us. If he does, he'll surely send that huge crab our way."

"Well, we can't stay hidden forever," Joshua said, shaking his head. "I mean, how will Epani find us? He's our only source of help at this point."

"He found us before," Andrew proclaimed.

Joshua shook his head. "But we were out in the open each time that happened. How will he find us if we're hidden? No, we have to go back."

"No!" Andrew declared, standing in front of Joshua. "It's too risky."

Joshua squared up against Andrew with his hands on his hips. Neither of them backed down.

"Well, the Kuelas, then," Joshua said. "If we go back to Kuela's Nest Island, Luana can call upon them to help us find the beast."

Andrew shook his head. "It's too risky, Joshua. We don't know how many of those things are flying about up there. We'd be spotted in a heartbeat trying to cross open water."

Joshua sighed deeply. Breaking eye contact with Andrew, he paced back and forth. "Well, what do you propose we do, then? We can't just sit here forever."

"Look, we're on Atoweena at the moment, right, Luana?" Andrew asked her.

She nodded.

"I think we should to get to the highest point on this island. That way, we stand a better chance of finding the beast. If we know where it is, we at least have the advantage."

Joshua stopped pacing. He turned to his friends. He knew, deep down, Andrew was right. It was the only plan they had and they had to do something. He dipped his head in surrender.

"Luana, what's the best way to get from where we are now to the highlands…the highest point on this island?" Andrew asked.

Luana turned, raising her arm to point in the direction Galleon and Sarah had come from.

Just at that moment, there was a piercing shriek. Everyone looked up to see another black Kuela flying overhead. They all ducked for cover, each finding a place to hide beneath the shrubs and leaves in the underbrush.

Nobody moved as the black Kuela continued to shriek. The noise wasn't getting farther away. It was circling above. Joshua's heart pounded so heavily in his chest, he thought it might burst right through. He tried to keep calm and remain silent. Waves of intense emotion ran rampant through his mind. Struggling to control his breathing, he thought he might pass out.

Then he felt the warm sensation of a hand reaching for him. It was comforting, like mother's embrace. Sarah entwined her fingers with his and gripped his hand tightly. Joshua caught her eye. She raised her hand gently up and down in front of her chest and mimed breathing in and out in unison, as if to encourage Joshua to breathe along with her.

Joshua tried to block everything out except for Sarah's face. He followed her breathing, taking long, slow, deep breaths along with her, all the while maintaining eye contact. In that moment, he felt himself lifted by her strength. His anxiety melted away.

After a while, the shrill of the Kuela faded. Before long, the hideous noise could no longer be heard at all.

Moments later, Joshua inched his head up through the leaves of the bush he was crouching beneath. Galleon, Andrew and Luana did the same a few paces away. Joshua and Sarah stood up, still hand in hand.

Joshua pulled Sarah towards him and wrapped his arms around her. They stood there in a warm embrace.

"Well, honestly!" Galleon exclaimed. "This place certainly keeps you on your toes, I'll say that."

Andrew climbed one of the trees to get as close as he could to the low canopy. Pushing the palm fronds to one side, he surveyed the skies, looking to see if the black Kuela was anywhere to be seen.

"Is it gone?" Luana asked Andrew, as he leapt back to the ground, losing his footing and stumbling in the process.

"It's gone," he said, picking himself up and brushing away all the leaves. "But who knows for how long. Come on. We should get going."

Taking point, Andrew strode out in the direction Luana had indicated. Everyone followed behind in single file.

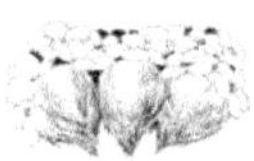

Several hours into the walk towards the highlands, Joshua was panting heavily. Even though his friend steered them a path that kept them shielded from the piercing sun, sweat poured down Joshua's face. *I haven't been drinking enough water.* He found himself unable to maintain pace with everyone, his legs barely able to keep him going as the group continued their ascent.

The centre of Atoweena was very rocky with volcanic outcroppings jutting out everywhere. Andrew insisted they avoid exposed areas. This added to the length of their push up to the higher elevations. The hike should have taken them an hour or two, but Andrew had them following a path through the thick island vegetation, meandering back and forth in an inefficient route. Although it made the journey that much more arduous, Joshua understood it was necessary to remain under cover. Several times they even had to double back to avoid walking too far out into the open. The threat of distant prying eyes loomed over them and they all knew it. Everyone kept a vigilant watch out for more black Kuelas.

"Andrew!" Joshua cried out, barely making any sound in his exhaustion. Just ahead of Joshua, Sarah heard the plea.

"Andrew, we need to rest," she called out.

Reluctantly, Andrew halted his advance and they all congregated under a palm tree. Everyone except Luana slumped to the ground.

"Here," Luana said, rummaging at the base of the tree. She plucked tufts of moss from its base and brought them over to where Joshua was panting heavily. "Lift your head up and open wide," she said, holding the clumps of matted green mass above his head.

He did as he was told. Luana squeezed the moss and a generous trickle of cool, clear water dropped into Joshua's mouth. He gulped it down quickly. She then squeezed some more of the soothing liquid onto his head and shoulders. He took in a deep breath and let out a satisfying sigh.

"Thanks, I really needed that."

The palm tree was a few paces from a rocky precipice. Andrew stood up and walked over to its edge. Peering down, he kicked a pebble over the rim. It took a long time to strike the ground below.

"Better not stray too close to the edge," Andrew said, taking his seat again. "It's a pretty long way down there. There's no way any of us would survive that fall."

Sarah stood up and inspected the root of the palm tree they had chosen to shelter under. "I think we could all use some of that fresh water Luana found," she said. She bent down and grabbed the only small clump she could see. "Hmm. There's not much moss on this tree."

Sarah squeezed what little water there was. It was barely enough for a mouthful.

"Here, let me help," Joshua said. He stood up and wandered off into the bush to find some more.

Sarah stepped towards the precipice.

"Not too close, Sarah." Andrew warned.

"Don't worry, I just want to take a…"

CRASH!

A figure came flying through the canopy and landed on Sarah. They both fell to the ground, rolling over and coming to rest at the edge of the cliff. Sarah and the figure struggled but before anyone knew what was going on, the assailant jerked the girl to her feet and stood behind her with a knife forced against her throat.

It was Kahu'niti. He was panting heavily. Gaunt and dishevelled, with claw marks across his face, he had a terrified look of panic in his eye. His arms and face were covered in dirt and blood. Tattered clothes hung loose from his body.

Galleon and Andrew both moved towards them.

"If anyone moves, I'll slit her throat!" Kahu'niti shouted, stepping back. As he did so, he knocked some pebbles off the cliff, sending them falling towards the rocky bottom. Moments later, the sound of them striking the rocks below echoed out.

Kahu'niti seemed possessed. His eyes darted to each of them and he pressed the knife so hard against Sarah's skin that blood trickled down the blade.

Andrew and Galleon both froze.

Andrew held his hands in front of him. "Okay, okay! Easy now, don't hurt her. What do you want?"

"Where is he?" Kahu'niti shouted. There was a tremor in his voice.

"Where's who?" Galleon asked.

"Him! The one He's looking for. Where is he? Tell me now or I swear I'll slice her pretty head right off."

"Okay, okay, please…calm down. You mean Joshua, right?" Galleon asked, nodding and raising his eyebrows. "Listen to me. He's not here. He was killed in the attack on the village."

Kahu'niti swung round to face Galleon, keeping Sarah in front of him. She whimpered. Tears rolled from her eyes as she strained to breathe under the force of the knife.

"You're lying to me. He's here, somewhere. I know he is. I've been tracking you."

"No, it's the truth," Andrew pleaded.

Galleon could see Joshua crouching behind the palm tree. He was out of Kahu'niti's line of sight but there was still a good distance between Joshua and the attacker. Galleon raised his hands in the air slowly.

"No! Listen to me. We're telling you the truth. He died during the attack on the village." As he spoke, Galleon crept sideways.

Kahu'niti turned in place to keep the Imp in front of him. The more Galleon moved, the more Kahu'niti moved with him and the more the man's back was turned towards Joshua's position.

Kahu'niti's breathing intensified. Beads of sweat trickled down his face. He shook his head.

"No, I don't believe you. You don't understand. He'll...He'll...He'll kill me." The desperate man sobbed. His whole body shook. "He'll make me kill again. I...I don't...I can't. Not again. Don't you understand? I have to. I have to kill him, or else—"

As Galleon continued to shift to the side, maintaining eye contact with the would-be murderer all the while. He stepped on a twig. It broke in two with a loud crack. Startled by the noise, the desperate man thrust the dagger out towards Galleon, relieving the pressure on Sarah's bloody throat.

"NOW!" Andrew shouted.

"ARRRGGGGHHH!"

Joshua lunged forward, flying through the air. The full force of his body struck Kahu'niti, knocking both him and Sarah to the ground. Joshua and Kahu'niti struggled on the forest floor. Andrew grabbed Sarah by the arm and pulled her away. Dust flew everywhere as Joshua and Kahu'niti struggled on the ground fighting. The madman rolled Joshua over. He bestrode him with his blood-stained hands at the young Woodsman's throat. Joshua gasped for air. Galleon lunged at them, knocking Kahu'niti over the edge of the precipice.

Kahu'niti's screams faded into the distance as he fell.

Galleon and Joshua leapt up and stumbled away from the edge of the cliff. Sarah was crying. She was in shock. Joshua comforted her with a warm embrace. "Shhhhh. It's okay. It's all okay. He's gone."

A few moments passed before the dust settled. Galleon and Andrew walked to the edge of the cliff and peered over. They squinted at each other.

"Where's the body?"

# CHAPTER TWENTY-FOUR
## *Mind Control*

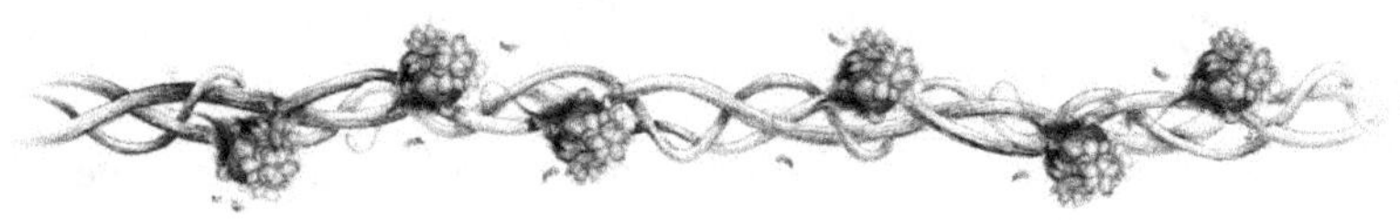

Not wanting to linger any longer than they had to, Joshua suggested everyone continue to move. "Luana, how much farther until we reach the peak?" he asked.

"It's not too far now. We'll be there before sundown if we keep up a good pace."

Although still shaken by her ordeal, Sarah put on a brave face. The physical wound on her throat was only minor but the terror would take longer to heal. She said very little for the remainder of the journey.

Even though everyone was on edge, the rest of the trek was uneventful. The group reached the summit as the sun was touching the horizon. It cast golden streaks across the ripples of the ocean under a crystal-clear sky.

Whilst Luana, Galleon and Sarah helped set up camp under the cover of a cluster of palms, Joshua joined Andrew in surveying the island. From beneath a single palm tree right at the very top of the hill, Joshua could see the whole island sloping below him in all directions. With the sun setting, the island cast a dark shadow to the east. Distant fires dotted the landscape like steam coming from a volcano.

"Village camp fires?" Andrew asked, squinting at the dozen or more plumes of smoke rising into the air.

Joshua shook his head. "I don't think those are campfires. I think they are the villages themselves on fire. Look."

Joshua pointed towards the closest plume of smoke. It was still too far away to make out any detail but a trail in the forest led away from the village towards the next plume of smoke. It looked like a scar on the landscape. He could make out more lines of destruction leading from village to village.

"I think that's the trail left by Hewa'luki as it's moving around the island. It's looking for us…for me." Joshua sighed deeply. He contemplated the trail of devastation below, shaking his head.

"Don't do this to yourself, Joshua," Andrew said, resting his hand on his friend's shoulder. "You didn't unleash that thing. The Goat did. He's the one responsible for all this, not you."

Joshua sighed again and shook his head. "Poor Luana. She'll be devastated to see this."

"Don't tell her yet. There's nothing she can do now anyway. Let her get some sleep. We can tell her in the morning."

Joshua nodded slowly.

"Come on," Andrew said quietly. "Let's go get some rest for the night."

They walked back to the others. By now, Luana was roasting Kea'hee nuts on a small fire. With the temperature dipping fast, everyone huddled by the flames, trying to keep warm. As the sun slipped below the horizon, the only sound was the crackling of the fire and the breeze drifting through the palm leaves.

Luana tended to a dressing she had prepared for Sarah's neck. Joshua reached into his keeper bag and pulled out the Orb of Sunshine. He held it up, feeling the markings etched on its side.

Joshua held the orb up to his face, beholding it. He marvelled at the imperfections in the fist-sized crystal glinting in the twilight. They captivated him. There was a strange elegance about it. Joshua couldn't quite put his finger on it. The orb was beautiful — mystical even.

As he continued to stare, the world around him faded. Joshua felt himself drifting away into another place. There was no sensation of movement, only a melting away of the awareness of his surroundings. Everything went blurry and indistinct. No longer sure of where he was, Joshua felt himself floating. Before him, a dark swirl slowly emerged, like a distant storm approaching. It twisted and distorted, all the while coming closer. The cloud formed the shape of a face. Then, it came into sharp focus. It was the Goat.

Joshua felt a wave of anger surging from within. The Goat's face tilted forward, revealing the whites of his dark eyes. They pierced back at Joshua through bushy eyebrows. A matted tuft of hair hung beneath the Goat's chin. Huge ribbed horns grew out from either side of the Goat's head. They were black and pointed forward. A callous smile crept across the creature's face.

"What do you want?" Joshua's mouth didn't move yet he could somehow speak. Joshua didn't hear or sense any response. Instead, the Goat squinted and pushed His head forward still further.

"You will not succeed." The Goat's mouth wasn't moving yet Joshua could hear His voice as clear as day. It echoed through his mind.

"I succeeded back in Forestium. What makes you think I won't succeed again here?"

The Goat's face contorted. His grin gave way to a scowl. The evil monster shook His head violently. The two menacing horns seemed so close they might tear at Joshua's face. The Goat's roar was deafening. The echoes died down and the Goat once again wore His wry grin.

"Do you see what you have done? The destruction I have wrought here. This is your doing, Joshua. How much more torment will you inflict on these people? Give me what I want and I will allow them to live."

"And what exactly is it that you want?"

The Goat raised his head. His eyes widened. There was a moment's pause before the despicable creature spoke again.

"You know what I want. You have one in your hand right now."

"Why do you want the orbs?"

Suddenly, Joshua sensed a wave of panic that seemed out of place. Then the realisation hit him. It wasn't his own. It was the Goat's. Something about the orbs scared the Goat. It scared him so much, the malicious beast feared for his very life.

"What are you so afraid of? Afraid you're going to die? Afraid I'm going to finally kill you?"

The Goat roared again, shaking his head violently. Then he peered at Joshua intently. He squinted, as if concentrating hard.

A jumble of images flooded Joshua's mind in quick succession. They came thick and fast, each lasting only briefly. He recognised himself in each of the scenes playing out in his head but the events were unfamiliar. He tried to push them aside but he was powerless to prevent the rapid onslaught. Joshua found himself moving from one memory to another.

There was a memory of a tall, dark figure bearing down on him holding a finger out and screaming. Joshua was frightened and crying. Although he sensed this wasn't his own memory, the feeling of fright and intimidation triggered by the memory in his subconscious felt very real indeed.

That memory lasted but a few seconds. It was replaced by another of him falling from a tree and breaking his arm. Again, Joshua had no recollection of ever having broken his arm but he felt a sudden rush of anxiety and pain flooding back as though the memory were real.

Next, he was falling into a river. There was a sudden rush of cold as he sank into the fast-moving torrent. He struggled to find the surface of the water. A feeling of panic and desperation overwhelmed him as teeth sunk into his arms, dragging him under.

Each memory triggered a different emotional reaction. Joshua's visions shifted from one memory to the next so fast, there was no time to think. His mind was being driven by pure instinct. He had no control over the emotions being generated each time a new vision flooded his mind.

He landed on a memory of himself looking into the Mirror of Prophecy. There, in the reflection, was the image of a young girl with feathers in her hair. The girl gasped for breath before falling silent and motionless. She was dead. *I've seen this girl before,* Joshua thought to himself. In the image, Joshua tilted her head so he could see who it was. He was horrified when he saw her face. It was Sarah. A wave of intense sadness flooded his mind. The emotion was overpowering. Joshua couldn't bear it. He tried to push it away but unlike the others, this memory wouldn't move. He found himself running through it over and over again in his mind. Then, the image switched. It was now Luana in the memory, repeating itself over and over. Each time, his anguish heightened still further.

Joshua's torment was tearing him apart on the inside. He was racked with grief at the belief he was somehow responsible for what he had seen. *If only I had killed the Goat before in Forestium when I opened the Portallas there*, he thought to himself. *I need to find and open the Portallas here*, he thought.

At that very moment, the image of Luana in the mirror faded. Joshua felt a wave of terror rush through him. It was a strange feeling, like it, too, didn't belong there. The fear was so intense, it overwhelmed him. *That's not my own fear. It's the Goat's!*

The feeling lasted briefly. It was supplanted by a new memory thrust into the forefront of Joshua's mind. This time, he was reliving the moment back in the village where Hewa'luki was rampaging, causing death and destruction everywhere it went. Joshua was forced to watch whilst the horrific beast sliced through flesh and bone of the islanders like a knife through butter. Men, women and children were being slaughtered everywhere he turned. He was powerless to prevent it. He wanted to reach out to them but he kept seeing the faces of the children screaming in terror. The torment Joshua felt was so overpowering it was going to kill him.

"Joshua! JOSHUA!"

Joshua opened his eyes to find Andrew's hands on his shoulders. Andrew was shaking him and shouting his name. Dazed, Joshua turned left and right before locking his eyes onto his friend.

"Are you okay? You've been frozen staring at that orb forever with tears running down your face. We couldn't snap you out of it."

Joshua panted heavily, taking in a huge lungful of air. After a few moments, he came back to his senses.

"Joshua, what happened to you?" Sarah asked. She took the Orb of Sunshine from his hand and placed it back into his keeper bag.

"It was Him. The Goat. I was with Him—somewhere. I...I don't know where. I could talk with Him...sense Him. It was like it was back in Forestium with the Orb of Vision. I could...I could sense His thoughts and feelings."

"What did you find out?" Galleon asked.

Joshua glanced around. His eyes landed on Luana sitting by the fire. She looked sullen.

"I..." Joshua paused mid-thought. The vivid memory of Luana's dead face reflecting back at him through the Mirror of Prophecy once again surfaced, sending his anxiety shooting.

"Well?" Galleon asked impatiently. "Out with it, young man."

Galleon followed Joshua's gaze over to where Luana was sitting. He then turned to look back at Joshua. Joshua's head sank.

"I...I need some time. It all...well, it all happened so fast. I need to gather my thoughts."

Galleon sighed. He stood up and put his hands on his hips. Joshua caught his eye. Galleon's eyes shifted to Luana and then back at Joshua. He nodded slightly. There was a curious expression on the Imp's face. Joshua thought he might understand.

Galleon walked back to his place by the fire, all the while keeping his eye on Joshua.

After several minutes, Joshua spoke. "He's afraid."

Everyone turned to him.

"Afraid of what?" Andrew asked.

"Of us. Of me. He's afraid we're going to open the Portallas in this world. The thought terrified him."

"Epani said something about that before," Luana said. "What did he say this Portallas was again?"

"I don't really know. Maybe it's…I don't know. I just know that we need to find the last orb and open the Portallas here. It's the only way we're going to stop him from continuing to kill all the people of Archipelago."

"At least we now know where to find the third orb," Andrew said.

"What do you mean?" Luana asked.

"Epani said it was within the belly of that huge Palm Crab."

"Yes, Hewa'luki. That's where we have to go next." Joshua said.

"But that thing could be anywhere." Luana said.

Joshua and Andrew caught each other's eye. Joshua opened his mouth to speak, to tell Luana about the devastation he and Andrew had seen earlier, but Andrew cut him off.

"Let's get some rest. It's been a tiring day for all of us. We'll see what we can find in the morning. I'll take the first watch. Galleon, you can relieve me in a few hours."

"Right you are," Galleon said.

# CHAPTER TWENTY-FIVE
## *Devastation Revealed*

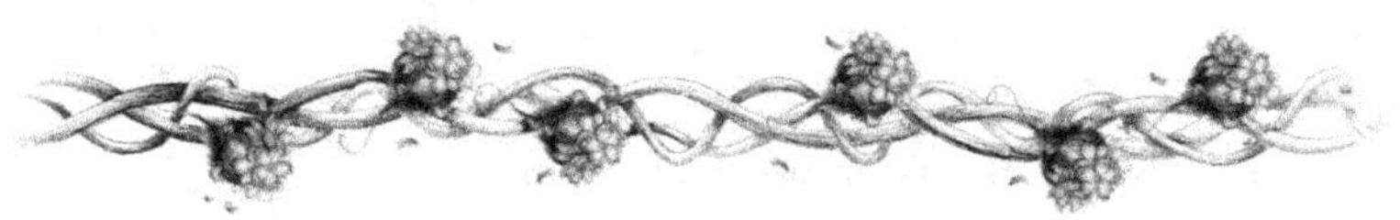

The next morning, Joshua awoke as the others were stirring. The mood in the camp was sombre. Standing up to yawn and stretch, he took in his surroundings. Far below them, the ocean was calm. Still waters in all directions glistened in the light of the rising sun. Before long, the camp was a hive of activity. Sarah was rummaging through a pile of berries. Galleon was prying sand out of his toenails. Andrew was prodding the fire back to life.

"Where's Luana?" Joshua asked, yawning.

Andrew looked at him and shrugged.

"Haven't seen her yet," Galleon said.

Sarah shifted over to where Luana slept. "She can't be far. It's still warm here."

Joshua walked over to the newly lit campfire. He held his hands over it and rubbed them together. There was a faint noise. He stopped and turned his head to listen. "What's that?"

Sarah looked up. "I hear it, too. It sounds like…crying?"

Andrew and Galleon both stood up. Joshua searched the camp, squinting and listening. He walked farther away until he found a large tree with a thick trunk. Joshua peered around the side of the tree. There, crouched on the ground, was Luana. Her head rested on her arms, which were wrapped around her knees. She was rocking gently to and fro, sobbing.

"Luana? What's the matter?"

"I think I know," Andrew said gently. Joshua turned to find Andrew beckoning him towards him. "Come and have a look."

Andrew led Joshua to where they had stood the night before. In the clear light of day, the true extent of the devastation left in the wake of Hewa'luki was laid bare. The scars left across the landscape by the monster were much more extensive than they had at first seen. They crisscrossed in every direction, all over the island. They could now see dozens of smoke plumes rising into the air. As they turned to survey the entire island, it was clear the beast had been busy all through the night. Joshua wondered whether anyone could still be alive.

"I had hoped we might be able to spot it from here," Andrew said, "but those paths cross each other so much, it's going to be impossible to follow its trail."

Joshua's attention was caught by a lone Kuela circling above. The bird flapped its wings, fixing its position in the sky for a moment and then glided towards the camp. Everyone watched as it navigated the thermal updraft, shifting its wings and tail to maintain a steady course. It came right into the camp and landed by the fire. Everyone stepped back some more. Before their very eyes, Epani took his human form.

"Hello, my friends," Epani said. His voice was calm—comforting, even.

Luana walked into the camp. Her eyes were red and puffy, her face expressionless. Epani walked over to her. He took both her hands in his.

"I cannot imagine the grief you must be feeling right now. I am sorry about your people."

A tear rolled down Luana's cheek. Her bottom lip quivered. Sarah walked over to comfort her.

"Epani, you must help us. We have to find Hewa'luki and destroy it. Have you been able to locate it?" Joshua asked.

"I know where it is," Epani said calmly. "A cave to the North of here. There is a network of old lava tunnels left over from the formation of this island. Finding the beast is not your biggest problem," he said, turning to Joshua. "That's the easy part. Killing it will be your challenge, Joshua."

"Where are these tunnels? I'll go alone."

Galleon turned to Joshua and said, "Alone? Are you mad? You wouldn't stand a chance on your own. What if…"

"Too many people have died already!" Joshua snapped, cutting Galleon off mid-sentence. "I'm not going to let any of you get hurt. I don't want anyone else to die because of me."

"It's suicide!" Galleon shouted at him.

"It's me He wants!" Joshua shouted back at him. "There's no reason to put any of you in harm's way."

"It isn't *you* He wants, Joshua," Galleon said, continuing with his defiant stance. "You said it yourself, He's afraid of you opening the Portallas. Don't you see? That's His weakness. That's how He can be defeated."

"Your friend is right," Epani spoke calmly. "Opening the Portallas *is* His weakness. With each new Portallas opened, the weaker He becomes."

"Right, and the only way to do that is to bring all three orbs together," Joshua said to Epani. "I have two but I need to get the third. You said yourself it's hidden inside Hewa'luki, so I need to go and…somehow defeat it." Joshua sighed. He cradled his head in his shaking hands. "I have to somehow kill it," he said, softly. "I have to make things right."

"*Somehow* kill it?" Andrew asked, walking up to Joshua and putting a hand on his friend's shoulder. "Sure, it sounds so easy when you put it that way. What do you think will happen to you if you come within sight of that thing? You've seen what it can do. No, I'm with Galleon on this one, mate. You can't just go off half-baked. We need a plan. Do you hear me?" He lowered his head to lock eye contact with Joshua. "*We* need a plan. We're *all* in this together. Don't ever forget that."

"Andrew's right," Sarah said. "Look, we're all going to need to put our heads together if we're going to stop this thing. You're not in this alone, Joshua." She took his hand. "We're all here for you. *I'm* here for you," she said, pulling him closer to her and clasping his hand tighter. "Together we're a team…right?"

Epani walked over to Joshua. He put his hand on Joshua's shoulder. "Listen to your friends, Joshua. You do not need to do this alone, my friend."

Joshua inhaled deeply, then slowly exhaled, puffing his cheeks. He did so again. After a few moments, he felt himself calming down again.

"So, what are we going to do? What's our plan?" Joshua asked Andrew.

Andrew sighed deeply. He shook his head.

Joshua turned to Epani. "You said Hewa'luki was resting in a cave."

"That is correct."

"And there's a network of tunnels there?"

"Yes."

"Is there any way of getting into the tunnels without being detected?"

Epani paused for a moment, regarding each of them in turn. Then he nodded. "There might be a way. But there are more dangers there than you know. The tunnels are infested with dark creatures."

"Well, I still have the orb of Sunshine," Joshua said. "It stunned the Palm Crab back on Ulaia Island where we met Kahu'niti. And I have the Dagger of Pa'hoa. I used it to kill two of them before."

Andrew and Galleon were both shaking their heads in disapproval.

"Look, if you have anything better, I'm open to suggestions," Joshua asserted. "Besides, the alternative—"

"The alternative," Luana said, speaking up for the first time since Epani arrived, "is to wait until every last man, woman and child on Atoweena has been murdered by Hewa'luki. And when it's done here…it will move on to the other islands."

There was silence as everyone pondered the magnitude of what Luana had just said.

"Well, then," Luana went on. "What are we waiting for? We have no time to lose."

# CHAPTER TWENTY-SIX
## *Panu'wahi*

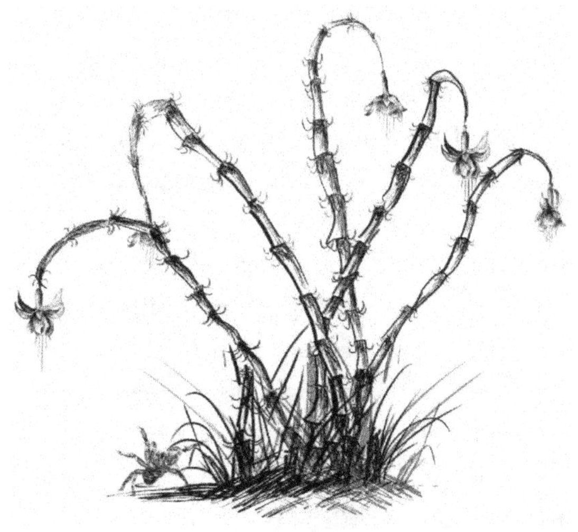

"Where did you say the tunnels were?" Luana asked Epani.

"To the north of the island. There is an area of barren rocks and tall prickly grasses. It is difficult terrain to travel through."

"Oh. You don't mean…Panu'wahi, do you?" Luana asked, a look of concern on her face.

"What is it, Luana?" Joshua asked.

"Well, it's just…we don't go there. It's teeming with venomous Ki'koohoi."

"Venomous what?" Andrew asked, leaning his head forward and raising his brow.

"Ki'koohoi. They're, um. Well, they're a sort of a, um…spider."

"Spiders? Did you say…spiders?" Galleon asked, his voice trembling. "I'm…ha, ha. Are…are you sure? S-spiders? R-really?"

Galleon shifted on his feet. He started scratching his arms.

"Don't tell me you're scared of little spiders, are you?" Andrew said, laughing.

"Oh, they're not small," Luana said.

"Say what?" Andrew said, turning sharply to Luana.

"They're not that small. They can grow quite big—much bigger than the palm of your hand. We stay away from them as much as we can. They can be quite aggressive if disturbed. A single bite can deliver enough venom to kill an adult. Death can come quickly—a matter of hours sometimes. We've moved entire villages away from the north side of the island to avoid coming into contact with them."

"Well, that certainly sounds to me like the ideal place for Hewa'luki to hide out," Sarah said.

"I've never seen these tunnels," Luana said. "Anyway, it isn't only the Ki'koohoi there we have to worry about."

Everyone's eyes were on Luana.

"There are Pana'malu palms there as well."

"You mean those trees that fire toxic darts?" Andrew asked.

Luana nodded.

"Oh great, that's just great!" Galleon huffed. "So, let me get this straight. All we have to do is somehow navigate the dangerous terrain of long, prickly grass in an area even the natives actively avoid; try to stay away from the types of trees that nearly killed me once already; and all the while trying to steer clear of monster-sized spiders that will kill us with a single bite? This is so we can find our way into and through a network of tunnels we know nothing about and not even Luana has seen, which are probably littered with vicious man-eating crustaceans, just so we can get close to a massive monster that's big enough to wipe out entire villages…and somehow kill it. Have I missed anything?"

"Yes," Andrew said. "We have to avoid the black Kuelas as well."

Galleon rounded on him, giving him a piercing stare. "Great!" he said, raising his hands in the air and turning to walk away. "That's just great. Honestly!"

"Don't worry about the Ki'koohoi," Luana added hastily. "They're quite easy to spot in the tall grasses. Although you do have to make sure you don't accidentally step on them."

"What do they look like, Luana?" Sarah asked.

"Their bodies are about the size of your fist with very long, hairy legs. If they feel threatened, they raise their front two legs to expose their fangs. Their black bodies show up quite easily in the long, brown grass, so we should be able to avoid them."

"Should?" Galleon scoffed.

"How well would those black bodies show up inside a dark tunnel?" Sarah asked.

Luana shook her head and said, "Like I said, I…I've never seen these tunnels, so…"

Galleon scowled.

"Don't worry, mate," Andrew said, walking over to the Imp and patting him on the back. "Just think of it as…an adventure. Think of all the stories you can tell everyone when we get back." He looked up and walked away muttering, "…if we ever get out of this place alive, that is."

"More like a bloody suicide mission if you ask me," Galleon huffed. "Honestly!"

"Right, then. Let's get going, shall we?" Joshua suggested.

"I will leave you now, my friends," Epani said. "I am more useful to you in the air, where I can keep a watch out for the Goat's dark creatures of the underworld. If I spot any, I will circle above your position…as a warning for you to take cover. If I can, I will also indicate where it is safe to enter the tunnels."

Joshua nodded. Epani stepped back and began his transformation. Moments later, a beautiful Kuela took off over the island.

# CHAPTER TWENTY-SEVEN
## *Ki'koohoi*

Luana and Joshua led the rest of the group down the northern slopes of Atoweena's highlands. The protection offered to them from the dense palm forest lasted only for a couple of hours. Around mid-morning, breaks in the canopy started to appear as the trees thinned out and the dense underbrush of shrubs gave way to tall grasses.

"Ouch!" Galleon yelled from behind. He was snagged on something and was struggling to free himself. His arms were flailing over his head but his face was hidden by a tangled mess of hair and grass.

"Wait," Luana called. "Don't pull on them, you'll just get more tangled. Here, let me help."

She walked back to where Galleon was struggling. He had somehow managed to get himself entangled with stalks of grass from all directions and was now thoroughly stuck.

"What is this infernal stuff anyway?" He kept trying to move his arms but Luana kept slapping him and telling him to keep still. There were scratches up and down his arms and across his face.

About a dozen grass reeds entangled him like a huge ball of knotted string. The golden-brown shoots extended up from the ground to about Luana's height. Along each stem were clusters of barbs. The stems thinned out towards the top, where the reed terminated with a blue and yellow flower. Protruding from the centre of each were thin, pointed needles. Several had broken off into Galleons head and arms, so Luana was carefully removing them.

"Ouch!"

"Will you stop moving! It's Kakula Grass. Here, hold still for a second and I'll show you how to remove it. See? Once the needles are out, you have to pull the barbs forward to remove the hook first. It's no use struggling. The harder you pull on it, the more entangled you'll become."

Andrew could barely contain himself. He was holding his sides from laughing. "You look like a bloody puppet, mate."

Galleon didn't seem to find any of it funny at all. "Honestly!" he scoffed. "I'm starting to think this place was designed just to kill Imps."

"There," Luana said impatiently, having removed the last cluster of barbs. "All better? Can we continue now?"

Before Galleon had a chance to reply, she turned and walked towards the front of the line, where Joshua was waiting for her at a fallen log. She took Joshua's hand and helped him over the obstacle. Sarah followed, keeping a watchful eye on the two of them.

"Come on, mate," Andrew said to Galleon, still laughing. "You walk in front of me. That way, if you get stuck again, I can be the first to stop and laugh at you."

Galleon turned and scowled at him before walking on. Andrew followed, still chuckling to himself.

"What did Luana call this grass?" Joshua asked Sarah.

"Kakula Grass," she replied. "I've been toying with it a little. Want to see something neat?"

"What do you mean?"

"Here, let me show you."

Sarah stopped to snap a reed from its base, and then they continued to walk. The bottom section of the reed was quite strong and hollow. She grabbed it with both hands on either side of the first cluster of barbs and broke it into two. The barbs remained attached to the top section, leaving the bottom section a simple, hollow tube. She then carefully removed some of the needles from the flower end and discarded the rest. "Watch this," she said.

Resting the needles inside one end of the hollow reed section, she held the other end to her mouth and then blew sharply. The needles launched from the end of the reed and went shooting through the air.

"Wow!" Joshua exclaimed. "That's clever."

"Well, I doubt it'll be of any use against Palm Crabs or anything, of course."

"No, I don't suppose so."

"I'm just hoping we don't run into any of those things. I hate them."

Luana caught up with them.

"Luana, you said before that the Palm Crabs attack every now and then?" Joshua asked.

"They invade one of the islands maybe once or twice a year," she nodded.

"That's horrible," Sarah said. "I'd hate to have to live with those things crawling around all the time."

"The problem is that we see them so rarely, it's easy to become complacent. Any one person could go years without seeing any. There are even some people on some of the remote islands that don't believe they exist at all. Youngsters in particular can be quite vulnerable. They don't get a chance to recognise the danger before…well, before it's too late."

"Ouch!" Galleon cried from the back of the group.

"I'll go and sort him out," Sarah said, chuckling.

"Is that what happened to your younger sister?" Joshua continued.

There was a long pause before Luana replied. She lowered her head and said softly, "It must have been. Before anyone knew what was going on, it was already too late. Kalena had been taken. Do you have any brothers or sisters?"

"Me? No. Well, I had a sister, but…she died at birth."

"Oh, I'm sorry to hear that."

"Yeah, well I was only a small child myself at the time—too young to understand even that I was going to have a baby sister. It was only very recently that I even found out about her."

"How did you find out? Did your mother tell you?"

"No. I, um, I saw it in a vision."

"A vision?"

"Yeah, well…you know those orbs?"

"Yes."

"Well, back in Forestium, where I come from, we have the Orb of Time. I had a…well, I'm not sure how to tell you. It was…an experience—an encounter."

Luana looked confused.

"Um…well, it's kind of hard to explain. It…showed me things. Things about my past. It showed me what happened when my mother gave birth to her. There was a battle going on at the time and…she…well, she didn't survive."

"Joshua, that's terrible." Luana put her arm around him.

"It was one of the hardest things I've ever had to deal with. The vision, I mean."

Luana squeezed Joshua a bit more. "It sounds like you've experienced quite a bit in life already. Nobody should have to go through things, Joshua. Nobody."

Luana was looking at Joshua reverently.

Just then, there was an ear-piercing shriek. In the distance ahead of them was a black Kuela flying towards them.

"Quick! Take cover!" he whispered as loudly as he dared. Everyone dove to the ground immediately. Sprawled out on his stomach, Joshua lay there with his hands in front of him. He arched his head up but couldn't see the black bird. The shrill noise it made continued to get louder. Once again, Joshua could feel his heart pumping. If the Kuela flew directly above them, it would surely spot something. He lowered his head and closed his eyes.

*Deep breaths, deep slow breaths*, he kept thinking.

Their only hope was to remain motionless and to hope the dark creature of the underworld didn't spot them.

The shrill of the black Kuela continued to get louder. Joshua tried his best to control his breathing and to keep as calm as he could.

Just as he had counted his fifth deep breath, he felt an irritation on his hand, like something was tickling it. It might be a bug or a fly but he resisted the urge to waft it away. Then he slowly raised his head and opened his eyes.

To his horror, crawling over the back of his hand, was a huge, black, hairy spider. Joshua felt his anxiety shoot through the roof but resisted the urge to move for fear of giving his position away to the black Kuela.

Against all his natural instincts, he held his hand rigid. The spider moved its legs slowly, dragging itself across Joshua's hand and towards his face. It was twice the size of his fist. It was so big, it covered Joshua's entire hand completely. Beads of sweat trickled down the young man's face. His mouth was open but he wasn't breathing.

The spider's legs were as thick as Joshua's fingers. Each black, hairy leg raised and lowered in turn as the creature crawled closer and closer to Joshua's face. It was so close, Joshua could see his reflection in the cluster of black eyes atop the creature's head.

Its front legs were within reach of his face when a fly landed on Joshua's eyelid. It made him blink, twitching his eye. The sudden jolt scared the spider. It raised its two front legs to reveal two curved, pointed fangs, dripping with venom. The black spider hissed, poised to jump. Paralysed with fear, Joshua wanted to scream, when…

*SWISH*!

A flight of needles flew past Joshua's eyes and impaled the spider, sending it toppling over. It lay on its back, motionless.

Joshua turned his head to the side. There, beside him, Sarah was lying with a Kakula grass tube still in her mouth. She lowered it and held her finger to her mouth, then pointed upwards. Soon the noise from the black Kuela faded. After a minute or two, it was gone. Joshua inhaled and exhaled deeply. He stared at the Ki'koohoi in front of him, green fluid dropping from the ends of the needles sticking out of it.

The others got to their feet — everyone except Galleon. He was once again entangled, and Andrew was trying to free him. It would have been quicker had it not been for Andrew's constant laughing as he tried to pull a stubborn cluster of barbs from the tip of Galleon's nose.

"Ouch!"

# CHAPTER TWENTY-EIGHT

## *Hidden tunnels*

With the black Kuela now gone, Joshua remained there on the ground momentarily. He marvelled at the dead Ki'koohoi spider and at how close he had come to death—again! A foot swished past and kicked the spider into the reeds. Joshua raised his head to see Sarah standing over him.

"Come on, there's no telling if that black Kuela will return," she said, reaching out a hand. She helped Joshua to his feet and the group continued on in a northerly direction.

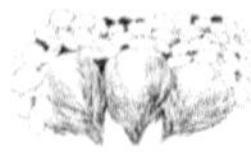

By midday, the sun was beating down on them. It was a clear and sunny day with not a cloud to be seen. Blue skies stretched as far as the eye could see in all directions. The highlands of Atoweena were now starting to fade in the distance behind them. The gentle whistle of the wind rushing through the swathes of Kakula grass was punctuated by a cacophony of insects.

The occasional song of a normal Kuela could be heard in the distance but the skies were otherwise empty. Every now and then, Luana would direct them away from a Pana'malu tree. In the tall grasses, they weren't that easy to see until you were right on top of them but Luana seemed instinctively to know where they were.

Every now and then, Galleon could be heard gasping and leaping to one side when he encountered another Ki'koohoi spider. He insisted on following so close behind Andrew, he kept stepping on his heels.

Joshua heard another colourful Kuela off in the distance. He followed this one's course through the sky. Instead of veering away, as all the other Kuelas had been doing all morning, this one meandered through the sky towards them. It continued to get closer before circling above a spot to the northwest of their current position.

"Luana," Joshua called ahead.

"I see it," she replied, also keeping her gaze locked onto the Kuela. "Let's head over there and see."

She changed direction and started towards the location where the Kuela was circling. When they reached the area, the Kuela flew off and was soon out of sight again.

"Are we there yet?" Galleon asked, probably for the fiftieth time.

"Not sure," Joshua said. "It could have been Epani. There's no way to tell. The ground is becoming rockier but I can't see anything through all this tall grass."

"Well, I can't see any entrances to no tunnels," Galleon complained. "I hope we find them soon. These damned Kakula barbs are killing me and I'm running out of bloody skin."

"This is the spot where the Kuela was hovering," Sarah said. "Maybe we should spread out?"

"Good idea," Andrew said.

Everyone split up and walked off in a different direction. Joshua bent down to pick up one of the rocks that the ground was strewn with. There were so many of them, it made walking quite difficult. The rock was black and jagged. It was light and full of holes.

After a few minutes of searching, everyone assembled again. Everyone, that is, except for Galleon.

"Wasn't he with you?" Joshua asked Andrew.

"I don't know. He couldn't stop stepping on me all morning and now he's gone and disappeared."

There was a faint call.

"Hold on. Can you hear that?" Joshua squinted, turning his head and trying to hear where the sound came from.

"I'm over here!" The voice called from afar.

"I hear it too," Sarah said. "It's coming from this direction." She walked off into the reeds and everyone else followed.

"Joshua! I'm over here!"

"I've found him." Sarah called out.

Joshua and the others found Sarah standing beside a hole in the ground. Joshua peered into the dark opening. There was Galleon, staring back up at them all.

"I think I found it," Galleon called up.

Andrew peered into the hole. "See, I told them you weren't useless."

"Oh, very funny, Andrew. Very funny. Honestly!"

Joshua and the others climbed down through the hole. One by one, Galleon helped them in. Inside, the walls and floor were made from the same volcanic rock Joshua had seen above the ground. There were large boulders throughout. The tunnel was barely tall enough to walk through but quite wide—enough for the whole group to move side-by-side. There was enough light coming through the hole for them to see up to where the tunnel turned a corner in both directions. Narrow shafts of light broke through smaller holes in the ceiling at various points but none were as big as the hole they had climbed through. Despite the heat outside, the temperature inside was cool. The sounds of their voices echoed off the tunnel walls.

"Which direction?" Andrew asked.

Joshua shook his head. "Let try this way," he said. Watching their footing carefully, they made their way through the tunnel.

"What are those things on the walls?" Galleon whispered. Every few paces, clumps of string hung on the walls. The strands were giving off small amounts of light. Galleon walked up to one to inspect is closely. He reached out to touch it. It was sticky. "Luana, what do you make of this?" he asked.

Luana studied it closely. "I'm not sure. I've not seen anything like this before."

"What are those little lights behind it?" Galleon carefully pushed the clump of luminous string to one side. There, on the wall behind it was a small cluster of lights moving slowly. Galleon took a quick step backwards. The lights stopped moving. He edged forwards again. Slowly, he reached towards the lights.

"It's a spider!" Galleon leapt back in a blind panic, stumbling to the ground in the process. Andrew helped him to his feet again. The Imp brushed himself down hysterically, muttering to himself. "Spiders! Why does it have to be bloody spiders? Honestly!"

"You seemed to have figured out what they were, Galleon," Andrew said, once again laughing at his friend's misfortune. "Those are clearly spider nests. See, like I said. You're not useless at all."

Galleon continued to brush himself down frantically, like he was trying to rid himself of invisible spiders crawling over his body.

"Galleon! Shhh!" Joshua said. "Listen! Do you hear that?"

The echo of Joshua's words faded. In the distance, there was a clicking sound. It sent shivers down Joshua's spine.

"Quick," Joshua whispered. "Take cover!"

Everyone scattered to find a boulder to hide behind. The clicking grew louder. Around the corner from the tunnel behind them, a pair of bright lights emerged. As they moved towards the group's hiding place, the sound bounced off the walls.

The beast stopped under the hole they came through. The shaft of light illuminated the unmistakable outline of a Palm Crab. It was huge—about the size of the hole they all came through. It climbed up the side of the tunnel wall right by the entrance and stopped.

The black beast raised one of its huge pincers and tapped around the edge of the opening, like it had sensed something. It then stopped moving. Joshua's heart pumped so loudly he worried the animal might hear it. Then, the beast climbed back down the wall and resumed scuttling towards them. Joshua held his breath and crouched down. The beast scurried right past them, disappearing around a bend. After a few seconds, the tunnel was once again silent.

Joshua and the others emerged from behind their bounders. Galleon stood up, again brushing himself down, as if to remove spiders from his body, although there were none. Atop his head, however, was a luminous mass of spider web.

"Um, Galleon?" Andrew said, raising his hand slightly. "Stop! Don't…move…a…muscle," he said slowly. Galleon froze with an expression of fright on his face.

"W…w…what is it," he said, nervously.

"Just…remain…very…still," Andrew whispered calmly. He stepped slowly up to Galleon, raised his arm to his side at about the level of Galleon's head, like he was going to strike him.

*SWISH*!

He slapped a spider and web to the side, clipping Galleon's head just enough with his hand to send him flying sideways.

"Ouch! What did you do that for?"

"Um…you don't want to know."

"Honestly!"

# CHAPTER TWENTY-NINE
## *Attack of the Palm Crabs*

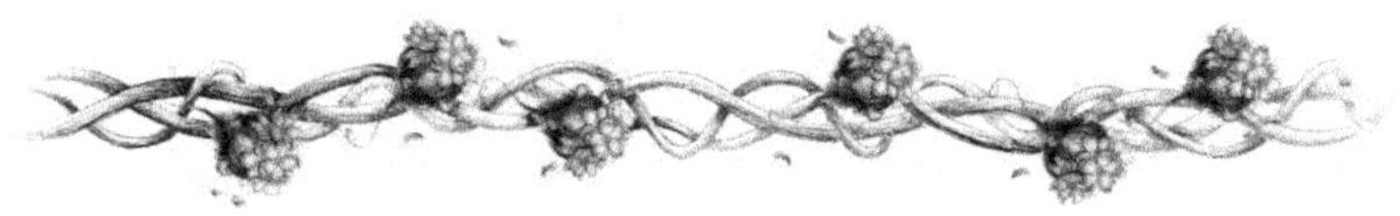

"Come on, we'd better keep moving before more of them arrive," Joshua suggested.

"Which way? W-w-what if we f-f-find more of t-them inside," Galleon stuttered.

"Just remember where we came from. If we need to, we'll have to make a run for it back to the entrance."

As they moved through the tunnel, Galleon kept jumping to one side each time he saw one of the luminous Ki'koohoi spider nests. In the dark tunnel, Joshua could make out the spider eyes shifting as they sidled past.

After they had crept through the tunnel for a few minutes, it opened up into a vast, empty cavern. Luminous spider webs all over the ceiling and walls lit up the cave enough to see about a dozen other openings leading away from the chamber. On the far side was a much larger tunnel opening — many times the diameter of all the others.

"It's not here," Joshua whispered.

"Well, that's good, isn't it?" Galleon whispered back. "I mean, that means it can't kill us, right?"

"It means it's out there, somewhere," Luana said in a hushed voice, "killing my people."

Joshua led the others out to the centre of the cavern. Their whispers bounced off the walls. Water seeped through the ceiling, dripping into small pools dotted throughout the cavern floor.

"Can you hear that?" Sarah asked.

"W-what? W-where? What can you h-hear?" Galleon asked, nervously.

"Joshua," Andrew said, "it's coming from you."

Joshua looked down at his keeper bag. There was a humming sound coming from it. He reached in and removed the Dagger of Pa'hoa. With his other hand, he pulled out the Orb of Sunshine. It was the orb that was making the humming sound. It pulsated with dim flashes of light.

"What does that mean?" Luana asked.

"I...don't know." Joshua said. He raised the orb to his face, studying it closely. A dim light flashed from within the orb every second or so.

There was a strange noise. The echoing of the chamber made it difficult to determine where it came from but it grew louder.

Then, from one of the tunnels, Joshua saw a pair of lights. They were much brighter than the spider eyes. As they came into view, Joshua's heart skipped a beat. Panic coursed through his veins.

Everyone huddled closer, creating a circle—all looking outwards from the centre of the cavern. Soon, more pairs of bright eyes emerged.

None of them came into the chamber. They remained at the tunnel entrances with legs raised and pincers snapping open and shut repeatedly. The frightening sound echoed off the cave walls.

Soon, there were dozens of pairs of eyes swarming around the tunnel entrances.

Standing there, with the Dagger of Pa'hoa in one hand and the pulsating Orb of Sunshine in the other, Joshua's gaze shifted from tunnel to tunnel. Eyes shone at them from each opening. The savage beasts were now crawling up the walls and ceiling with more lining up behind them.

"Why aren't they coming at us?" Andrew asked.

"I…I don't know," Joshua said. "Maybe they're afraid of something."

The stand-off continued until one of the beasts scuttled into the chamber. Joshua turned to keep it in front of him. The thorny beast crawled sideways along the wall of the chamber, getting closer.

Joshua held the Dagger of Pa'hoa out in front of him, waving it from side to side. Another creature crept towards the group from one of the opposite tunnels. Then a third joined them. The three beasts scurried around, encircling the group. They spiralled towards the centre of the cavern. Two of the beasts made a break for it and hurtled towards the group.

"JOSHUA!" Screamed Sarah. One of the animals lunged at her. She kicked at it with her foot but it latched onto the tip of her boot with its pincers. Joshua quickly ran around to the rear of it and thrust the Dagger into its shell. The vicious creature released Sarah's foot and started shaking violently. Light emanated from cracks in its shell, growing outward from the dagger's point of entry. With an ear-piercing shriek, the Palm Crab exploded, with body parts flying off in all directions. They ricocheted off the walls before falling to the ground.

There was another scream. This time it was Luana. Andrew was helping her fend off one of the other two attackers. Again, Joshua rushed over. He lunged at the beast and impaled it with the dagger. That animal also flew apart, squealing as it exploded. The one remaining Palm Crab backed away from the group towards the edge of the cavern again. Many of the creatures at the tunnel entrances had their claws in the air, tapping them against the cave wall. The terrifying sound bounced around the cavern.

"They're testing us," Joshua said. "That's what they're doing. They're trying to find a weakness."

All the tunnels were teeming with eyes shifting in the dark. With no way to escape from the cavern, Joshua thought hard, considering his options. The dagger could kill them but there were so many, it would be impossible to kill enough of them and manage to get everyone out.

Two more pairs of eyes came towards them. These were followed by another three. Still more came with others following behind. Soon, Palm Crabs were scuttling all around them. More kept coming out of the tunnels. They were crawling up the walls and over the ceiling. Dozens of the bloodthirsty animals closed in on the group in the centre of the cave.

The Orb of Sunshine in Joshua's hand pulsated more intensely. The flashes of light quickened as they got brighter. Still more vicious animals came pouring through the tunnels and into the cavern. They were almost upon the group when there was a blinding flash from the Orb of Sunshine. Shards of brilliant, white light exploded from it. They shone right into the eyes of the Palm Crabs. The blinding light lit up the cave so much that everyone had to cover their eyes.

The advancing animals stopped dead in their tracks. Those in the tunnels scurried away but those struck by the shards of light all started the shake violently.

The cave rang out with squeals. Each pair of eyes stopped moving. The light from the orb subsided. After a couple of seconds, it went out altogether and the orb was silent again.

CRASH!

Each of the fifty or so Palm Crabs collapsed to the ground. Their eyes were no longer shining and they were not moving. The only noise in the cavern was the dripping of water into the pools.

Joshua stood there, his jaw dropped and eyes wide. As his terror subsided, he found himself panting heavily. The dagger and orb still in his hand, he glared at all the motionless animals.

He slowly lowered his hands and stood up straight. Creeping forward to one of the motionless creatures before him, he leaned towards it. It was standing lopsided, its shell held up by just two of its legs. He reached out with his foot and nudged it. The two legs buckled and the creature collapsed to the ground. Joshua jerked back.

"Are t-they d-dead?" Galleon asked, trying to overcome his fear. Like Joshua and the others, he was panting heavily.

"I think so, or maybe just stunned. I don't know." Joshua replied.

Andrew walked out to one of the creatures and pushed. It, too, collapsed to the ground and remained motionless. "What happened? I thought we were all going to be killed for sure."

"Yeah, so did I," Joshua said. "A good job we had the Orb of Sunshine with us."

"What did you do to activate it?" Andrew asked.

"I don't know. I mean, I didn't do anything. I think it activated when the Palm Crabs got too near it."

Joshua turned to the others. "Luana, Sarah, are you two okay?"

They both nodded.

"So, what now?" Galleon asked.

"We still need to find Hewa'luki," Joshua said, stashing the dagger and orb back into his keeper bag. He surveyed the cavern before pointing at the large tunnel. "That way," he said.

Joshua led the others out of the cavern and into the large tunnel. They walked for two or three minutes until Joshua could see the tunnel brightening. They turned a corner to see the opening of the tunnel ahead of them. It was overgrown with bushes and reeds. Clambering over boulders, Joshua led them all up and out of the tunnel. Once they were outside, Joshua saw a trail of fallen trees leading away from them.

"Luana, do you know where we are? What's in that direction?" He asked, pointing at the freshly carved path of destruction.

"Um, I think so. If I'm right, there's a small village called Haluku about an hour from here. It's where my sister and I were born. That's where it happened—that's where Kalena was taken from. I'm not sure, since we don't really visit this part of the island much."

"Great," Joshua said. "Let's head for there. Hopefully, we can catch up with Hewa'luki before it reaches the village."

Suddenly, there was a loud shriek behind them. Everyone turned to see what it was. There, perched atop the entrance to the tunnel was a black Kuela. It flapped its ragged wings and took to the air, flying away and out of sight.

# CHAPTER THIRTY
## *The Battle at Haluku*

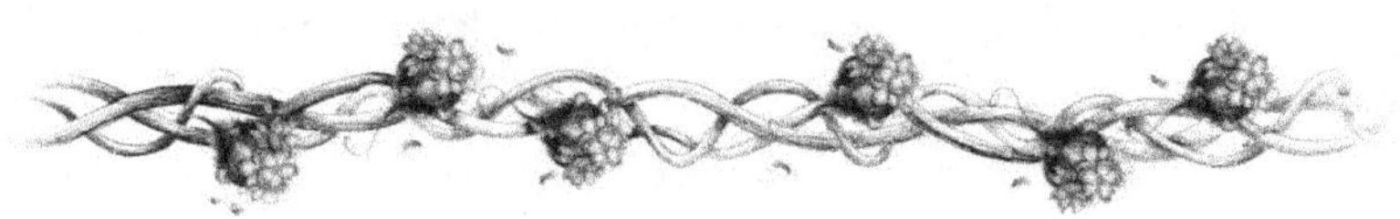

Water dripped down the dark walls of the rocky, spider-infested tunnel. Kahu'niti sat there huddled in the dark. His arms were wrapped around his knees. Ragged looking, with torn clothes, the dishevelled man crouched there, expressionless. His arms and legs were bloody. Makeshift bandages stained with blood and pus dangled from his limbs.

Shivering from the cold, he rocked rhythmically to and fro, muttering to himself. A Palm Crab scuttled towards him but he barely took any notice of it. The hideous creature stopped before him and crouched down, resting its shell on the ground so that its eyes were level with Kahu'niti's. The troubled man glared at it through bloodshot eyes. The crab's eyes lit up and shone straight into Kahu'niti's. As if powerless to resist, he stared into the bright lights. As he did, the cave around him seemed to drift away. He felt himself floating in a dark space.

The Goat peered at the man through menacing eyes. A hideous grin spread across His face.

"I have located the boy. Do you remember the girl I forced you to kill? He is heading for her village right now. You will go there…and kill him."

With a sharp intake of breath, Kahu'niti struggled but couldn't avert or close his eyes. He was utterly under the spell of the Goat.

"No, I won't…I…I won't do it. You should have let me die back at the cliff. You can't…"

The Goat's face contorted. He shook his head violently. Kahu'niti's eyes widened still further.

"You are no good to me dead…yet. You *will* do as I command," the Goat cackled with an evil grin. "Fail me again, and I will destroy every last island of this world."

Without thinking, a memory flooded Kahu'niti's mind. It was his memory of him killing Luana's baby sister at the Goat's command. The memory replayed in Kahu'niti's mind over and over. He struggled to close his eyes; to shut the memory out; to escape from this torture. Hard as he tried, he could not. The Goat roared with laughter. His face faded from view and Kahu'niti found himself once again rocking to and fro on the floor of the dark tunnel. The lights from the crab's eyes faded. The foul creature rose onto its eight spiny legs and backed away from Kahu'niti. The frail man stood up. He looked left and right before heading off down the tunnel. The dark creature scurried after him.

Luana led the group towards Haluku. By the time they arrived, they found Hewa'luki rampaging through the village. People were running about screaming. Huts were ablaze. A tall, muscular man came running out of the village. He was an imposing figure. A blood-stained spear was in his right hand. Tattoos adorned his arms and shoulders.

"Luana?" the man called out when he spotted the group.

"Paleki?" Luana replied. "What are you doing here?"

"I came as fast as I could. The Kuelas informed me the beast was here. I'm so glad to see you alive. I feared the worst when the beast attacked Hulawei."

"My friends and I only just manage to get away. We've been to where the beast lives. There are lava tunnels to the north. That's where it hides."

Two Palm Crabs emerged through the palm trees behind them. Paleki thrust his spear at one of them. It shot straight through the attacking animal's head. The crustacean stopped moving and collapsed to the ground. Paleki yanked the spear free and again and stood between the group and the other thorny beast. Joshua reached for his keeper bag but by the time he found the Dagger of Pa'hoa, Paleki had already dispatched the second beast.

A third crab came running at Joshua from the side. Without thinking, Joshua lunged at the thorny beast and thrust the dagger into the top of its shell, exploding it into hundreds of pieces.

Paleki watched with his jaw dropped and said, "This is the Dagger of Pa'hoa. How did you come by it?"

"It was given to me by the Oracle."

"The Oracle?"

"The Flame of Eternity," Luana said.

There was a scream coming from the village.

"Quickly," Paleki said to Joshua. "Bring the dagger with you!"

Joshua and the others all ran after Paleki into the village.

Through the trees, the true extent of the destruction caused by Hewa'luki was laid bare. There were dozens of bodies strewn about the place and few huts remained intact.

Villagers ran back and forth chasing after Palm Crabs with spears. Some of the attacking animals had severed limbs between their claws. Joshua stood there with the Dagger of Pa'hoa, looking for a target.

Just then, a grove of trees was pushed to the ground as Hewa'luki came crashing through. Scurrying between its feet were over a dozen crabs, many with blood dripping from their pincers. Hewa'luki's laser beam eyes scanned the clearing before locking on to Joshua. It then raised its enormous claw into the air.

All the animals at its feet scurried off to its left and right. They encircled the clearing, separating Joshua from the rest of the group. Several crabs fended off Paleki and the others. None of them came near Joshua, who was now isolated in the middle of the clearing. He was encircled by an impenetrable array of clacking animals with Hewa'luki bearing down on him—isolated and trapped.

Joshua held out the dagger in front of him and peered into the eyes of the giant beast. Joshua wondered what was happening and why they weren't attacking him. Then he remembered what happened back at the cave. He fumbled for his keeper bag and pulled out the Orb of Sunshine, which immediately began to pulsate.

Then out of nowhere, a figure lunged at Joshua from the side. It was Kahu'niti. The orb in Joshua's hand went flying, landing several paces away. It stopped pulsating. Joshua tried to reach for it but Kahu'niti dragged him back into the centre of the clearing. He then kicked Joshua's other hand, sending the Dagger of Pa'hoa in the other direction.

Joshua and Kahu'niti wrestled on the ground. Joshua kept reaching for the orb but Kahu'niti knocked him back each time. The two fighting men clambered to their feet and continued to struggle. Joshua kicked Kahu'niti in the side of the leg. The ragged man wailed and fell onto one knee.

Joshua searched for the orb. There it was, a couple of paces away. He reached for it. Suddenly, there was a piercing pain as Kahu'niti thrust a knife into his shoulder. Joshua screamed in agony and fell to his knees, holding the handle with one hand. Blood oozed from the wound.

Kahu'niti struggled to his feet. He staggered to where the Dagger of Pa'hoa was lying on the ground. Reaching down, he picked it up and staggered backwards towards Hewa'luki. He stood there beneath the giant's belly and caught his breath.

Joshua struggled to his feet, barely able to stand, still clutching at the knife in his shoulder.

"And now," Kahu'niti said, breathing unevenly and unsteady on his feet, "it is time…for you…to finally die."

Joshua scanned the perimeter. The solid barrier of Palm Crabs was still keeping everyone else at bay, including Paleki, Luana and the others. Nobody was able to come to his aid. He reached the knife stuck into his shoulder. With a swift tug, he yanked it out and placed his palm there, trying to stem the bleeding.

Wincing in agony, he turned to Kahu'niti. "Don't do it."

Kahu'niti shook his head. "You don't understand. You can't possibly understand. I have to be free of this torment. If I don't —
"

"You'll never be free!" Joshua shouted. "He'll never release you. Don't you see? He'll just keep using you. It's what he does. You must trust me, Kahu'niti. The only way out is to kill Him. Together we can do this. Help me kill Him. It's the only way you'll be free."

There was a noise from above. Circling over the village were half a dozen black Kuelas, shrieking fiercely.

"Listen to me, Kahu'niti. Listen to me carefully. So long as He continues to live, you'll never be free of this torment."

Kahu'niti stared at Joshua. His bottom lip quivered.

"You don't understand…what I've done…what I'm…capable of doing." His voice was broken. Tears rolled from his eyes. "I never wanted to do it. I never wanted to kill her. I tried to resist. But he's so powerful." He was now sobbing, his body shaking all over.

"And he'll make you do it again. Help me, Kahu'niti. Help me to help you. Together, we can put an end to all of this."

Kahu'niti closed his eyes. He screamed loudly. Then, with all the strength he could muster, he thrust the Dagger of Pa'hoa straight up and into the belly of Hewa'luki. The beast let out a shrill cry so loud, Joshua had to put his hands tight over both ears. The creature shook, with cracks forming from its belly, spreading out in all directions. Blinding light poured from each fissure. With an almighty eruption, the beast exploded, with shards of shell flying off all over the village. Everyone was blown to the ground.

# CHAPTER THIRTY-ONE
## *The Orb of Flight*

Joshua lay there until he could hear no more debris landing. Everything was quiet. His eyes were squeezed shut and his hands pressed against his ears. In that brief moment, there was nothing. No light, no sound—nothing. He couldn't even feel the pain from the knife wound. All Joshua could feel was his heart, still pounding. Joshua wanted the moment to last forever. There would be no more Goat, no more battles, no more dark creatures of the underworld, no more fighting, no more pain and no more misery.

The tranquillity lasted but for a brief time. His senses revived. He felt the sharp pain in his shoulder, and he opened his eyes. The dust was settling. Joshua peered upwards. There, looking down on him, were Sarah, Andrew, Galleon, Luana and Paleki.

Andrew and Sarah helped Joshua to his feet.

"Here, let me take a look at that," Sarah said as she tended to his wound.

Joshua checked the sky but the black Kuelas were nowhere to be seen. A few ragged black feathers were still floating to the ground.

"They're gone," Galleon watched the black feathers drift to the ground. "So are the Palm Crabs. Scurried back to those bloody tunnels, would be my guess. None left alive here anyway."

Joshua noticed Kahu'niti laying on the ground, face down.

"Is he —"

Paleki walked over and knelt next to Kahu'niti.

"He is alive," Paleki shouted. He helped Kahu'niti to his feet.

Kahu'niti looked dazed and confused. "Where am I? What's going on? What am I doing here?"

"Look," Joshua said, pointing to the ground next to Kahu'niti.

Paleki reached down and picked up a clear, spherical crystal. Standing up straight, he studied it before passing the orb to Joshua. "It is the Orb of Flight," he said with great reverence.

Joshua took the orb, holding it up to his face. Carved into one side was the unmistakable outline of a bird's wings.

"How do you know what it's called?" Joshua asked.

"I am the Protector of Atoweena, my young friend," he said, winking at Joshua. "You do not think I became this without being learned, now do you? It is written in the sacred scrolls. Legend tells that the Orb of Flight is a most wondrous thing. It can take you great distances—like a bird."

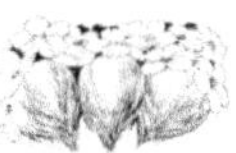

The Goat fumed with rage, his face contorting with anger at the failure of his plan to kill Joshua. He looked up into the vaulted ceiling in His dark room and howled.

Suddenly, there was a rumbling sound. The ground shook.

"What's happening?" Galleon shouted.

"It's Lua'pele," Luana shouted, pointing to the east. "It's going to erupt."

"We need to leave!" Joshua shouted, as the rumbling continued.

"LOOK!" Andrew yelled, pointing in the direction of the massive volcanic island.

An enormous plume of smoke launched out from the caldera. Clouds of ash, smoke and bounders shot up into the sky.

"QUICKLY! We have to leave! NOW!" Joshua shouted.

"There's no time," Paleki shouted. "The entire island is about to blow."

Joshua looked at the Orb of Flight. The he looked up and saw Luana staring at the plume of smoke thickening above the island.

She was facing away from him. Tied into her hair, Joshua saw three colourful Kuela feathers.

"Luana, quickly. Give me one of your feathers from your hair. I have an idea."

Luana pulled one of the feathers from her head and handed it to Joshua. He held the feather against the orb and an intense beam of light shot up into the sky.

Within seconds, Kuelas came flying over the treetops towards the light. There were dozens to begin with but they kept coming. Soon there were hundreds and then thousands. The enormous flock of colourful birds swarmed around the group in circles. They flew faster and faster—much faster than any Kuela would normally fly.

A vortex surrounded the group, forming ripples in the air around them. Everything distorted. It was like looking through water. Their view of the village went blurry. The vortex swirled so violently, it lifted trees into the sky, yet the air where they were standing inside was calm—hardly moving. Everyone looked around, unsure of what was happening.

Luana screamed.

The ground beneath their feet dropped away rapidly. It continued to fall, leaving everyone floating in the air. The view of Atoweena receded beneath them.

There was a loud swishing sound as the island kept moving away. The thousands of Kuelas continued circling them so fast it was difficult to make out any individual bird. Joshua looked down to see the island move to one side, replaced by the ocean. Then, another island appeared. It rose up towards them at high speed.

*SMASH*!

# CHAPTER THIRTY-TWO
## *Opening the Portallas*

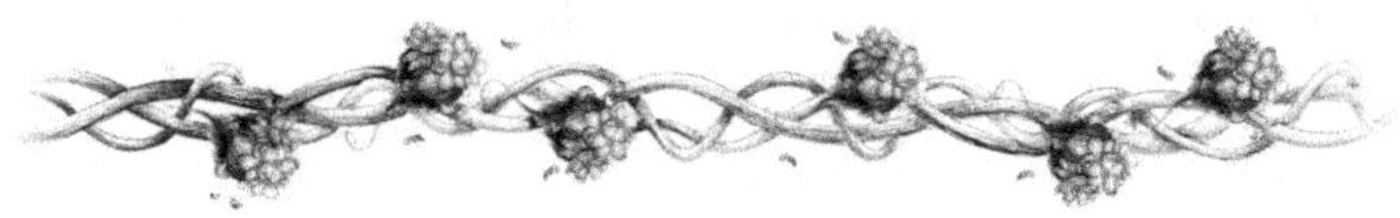

Once again, Joshua found himself lying on the ground with his eyes closed and his hands held over his ears. Once again, the only thing he could feel was his own heart beating in his chest. *What just happened? Did I dream it?* He opened his eyes. He was lying on a sandy beach. Just a few paces away, the crystal waters of the ocean shimmered in the evening light. All of the others were there with him, getting to their feet.

"Is everyone okay?"

"Well," Galleon said, brushing himself down. "If that doesn't clear your sinuses, I don't know what will."

"Where are we?" Andrew asked.

"I think we're on Kuela's Nest Island," Luana said.

Just out to sea, Joshua could see the top of K'pia poking up through the water.

"Look!" Sarah shouted, pointing to the east.

Joshua spun around. Across the rocky island, he could see the volcano on Lua'pele erupting in the distance. Plumes of smoke mixed with trails of red lava spewed out over the islands. The debris flew so high, it reached as far away as Atoweena and

Kihala's western beaches. Some of the eruption even reached as far as Ulaia. Molten lava trickled down the slopes of the Lua'pele caldera.

Paleki put his arm around Luana's shoulder. Tears rolled from both their eyes.

Joshua sank to his knees. He looked down at the ground. Anger welled from the pit of his stomach. "It was His doing. He'll never stop…not until someone stops him."

"Joshua?" Andrew said. "I've seen that look in your eyes before. What are you thinking?"

"I have all three orbs. Epani said the Goat grows weaker with each new Portallas opened." He reached into his keeper bag, pulled out the three orbs and laid them onto the sand between his knees. "The Orb of Sunshine and the Orb of Flight have both already been activated. I just need to activate the Orb of…Sacrifice."

"Joshua?" Andrew's voice changed. There was concern in his tone. "You're not thinking of doing anything stupid, are you?"

"I can't let this go on. I can't let Him continue to kill. I have to activate the orb myself."

He reached into his keeper bag and pulled out the Dagger of Pa'hoa.

"Joshua? NO!" Sarah shouted. "You can't do it. Please, Joshua! Put down the dagger."

Joshua continued to look at the blade in his hand. He shook his head. "I have to activate the orb to open the Portallas. It's the only way He can be defeated."

Luana ran forward and grabbed the Orb of Sacrifice from Joshua. Backing away from the beach, she said, "No, Joshua. I can't let you kill yourself. You've been through too much to die now."

Chills ran down Joshua's spine when he heard the unmistakable sound of clacking pincers. Through the trees behind Luana, a Palm Crab emerged and scurried towards her. It was a particularly large one with its claws held high in an aggressive posture.

"Luana, move away! Quickly!" Paleki shouted. He grabbed his spear in his right hand and held it poised to launch at the advancing beast.

Joshua got to his feet. "Luana! Listen to him. Move away! NOW!"

Luana continued moving backwards towards the Palm Crab. It sped closer to her.

"Please take care of yourself, Joshua."

"LUANA, NOOOOO!"

The creature thrust its claw into Luana's back with such force that it came out through her chest, dripping with blood. Paleki launched his spear. It struck the animal fiercely and knocked the beast backwards.

Joshua rushed forward. Luana collapsed in his arms. He sank to his knees, cradling her. "Noooooo!" he cried, tears streaming from his eyes. He looked down at young woman. Her eyes closed and her head fell lifeless to one side. Two colourful feathers were tied in her hair—exactly as the Mirror of Prophecy showed him back in Morelle.

Joshua lowered his head and continued to sob. Sarah, Galleon, Andrew and Paleki all came over and knelt beside him. They each put their hand on him and everyone grieved for Luana.

Then Joshua noticed the Orb of Sacrifice, still clutched in Luana's hand, was now pulsating. Her death had activated it. Joshua carefully laid Luana onto the ground. He removed the pulsating orb from her hand and took it over to where the other two orbs still lay in the sand.

He fell to his knees and placed the orb in contact with the other two. All three pulsated. They all flashed in unison. The pulses of light intensified. Joshua and the others got to their feet and backed away from the vortex that was now forming above the orbs on the beach. The swirling disturbance continued to increase as the Portallas opened. Through the vortex, Joshua could see many of the people from Morelle on the other side. Then his mother came into view. She smiled at him. A wave of emotion overcame Joshua and a tear welled in his eye.

Then, his mother was pushed aside violently. The Goat stepped into view. A menacing grin formed across the Goat's face. Joshua felt anger welling from deep inside him. The evil monster peered at Joshua through his bushy eyebrows.

"Your people will never be allowed to return to their world," he said slowly. "They will die, like she did. I will kill them all."

Joshua's anger swelled. He stepped forward. With all his might, he wanted to kill the Goat.

Then Paleki launched his spear through the Portallas, yelling "FOR LUANA!" It shot straight at the Goat and sank right into the evil creature's chest. The Goat let out an ear-splitting roar, shaking His horned head violently before He faded out of view. Then, Joshua saw the people of Morelle behind him, including his mother, fade from view. They were gone—freed.

Joshua once again sank to his knees, clutching at the wound on his shoulder. He looked up at the Portallas. Suddenly, everything went dark. The sensation lasted but for a moment. Then there was a blinding flash of light. Joshua found himself floating inside a flame. He was hovering above the sand. The flame that engulfed him wasn't moving. It was frozen all around him. He could see Paleki and the others there on the beach beside him but they, too, weren't moving. It was as if time had stopped still. A voice echoed from within his mind. The Oracle's voice was sweet and soothing.

"My dear Joshua. Your bravery and courage has freed your people. Their pain and suffering is at an end."

"My people?" Joshua asked. His lips didn't move but he could somehow communicate with the Oracle. "They're safe? Are they…back in Morelle?"

"Your people are once again of their world. It is your doing."

"You knew all along, didn't you? You knew that Luana was going to die. Why didn't you tell me?" Joshua felt a wave of guilt overcome him. "I could have saved her. She shouldn't have died because of me." His remorse at her death sent waves of sadness coursing through his veins.

"My dear Joshua, I told you only the truth. The Orb of Sacrifice demanded a life. That was the price you had to pay." There was a pause before the Oracle spoke again. She whispered softly, "She must have cared for you deeply, for only that could have called forth the power of the orb. Honour her. Honour her memory. Live your life well, Joshua. Live your life full. Live the adventure she would have wanted for herself."

Joshua strained against the intensity of his own emotions.

"Is He dead?"

"The one that wields the power…still lives. Your paths…will cross again."

Struggling to hold back the tears, Joshua asked, "How can we get home?"

"My dear Joshua, you have the power with you to return to your world. You have the Orb of Flight. Use it well. We will speak again."

The Oracle's voice echoed before fading away from Joshua's mind.

There was another blinding flash of light. Joshua found himself kneeling on the ground. The three orbs were in front of him. They were no longer humming and no longer pulsing with light. He picked them up and placed the Orb of Sacrifice and Orb of Sunshine into his keeper bag but he kept hold of the Orb of Flight.

Joshua stood and looked down at Luana. A tear rolled down his cheek. Sarah took his hand and squeezed it tightly.

"You have saved us all, my friend," Paleki said, walking over and resting his hand on Joshua's shoulder. "Hewa'luki is dead. Our people are once again safe. We are forever in your debt."

Joshua peered into the Protector's eyes. He strained to speak through his intense grief. His bottom lip quivered. "But at what cost?" he said, shaking his head and peering at Paleki through water eyes. "Luana is dead. So many of your people are dead."

Joshua lowered his face and shook his head. Sarah clasped him around the shoulder and rested her head against his.

Paleki nodded and lowered his head. "It is true. Luana's sacrifice was…unfortunate. But her memory will live on. We will cherish all that she was. She will not be forgotten."

"We have to leave you now," Joshua said with a tremor in his voice. He looked down at Luana lying on the ground. He knelt down and kissed her tenderly on her forehead. "I'm so sorry,

Luana," he said. Another tear rolled from his eye and dropped onto Luana's face. "I will never forget you."

Joshua took one of the feathers from her hair. He stood up and addressed Paleki. Holding his fist to his chest, he bowed before the Protector. Paleki did likewise.

Joshua and the others took a step back. He took the feather and held it against the Orb of Flight. An intense beam of light shot up from the orb into the sky.

Kuelas by their thousands emerged from all directions towards the beacon. As they swooped in, they circled around Joshua, Sarah, Andrew and Galleon. The birds flew so fast, they became an indistinct vortex of colour. The air around them distorted. Joshua saw Paleki standing there looking down at Luana's body, his head bowed in respect.

Everything receded as the entire beach and island dropped away. Joshua and the others were suspended in the calm air inside the vortex as the thousands of Kuelas continued to race around them in a blur. The island dropped until it was out of sight. The vortex intensified. Joshua felt dizzy. His vision blurred and he felt everything drifting away. Everything went dark.

Christopher D. Morgan

# Epilogue

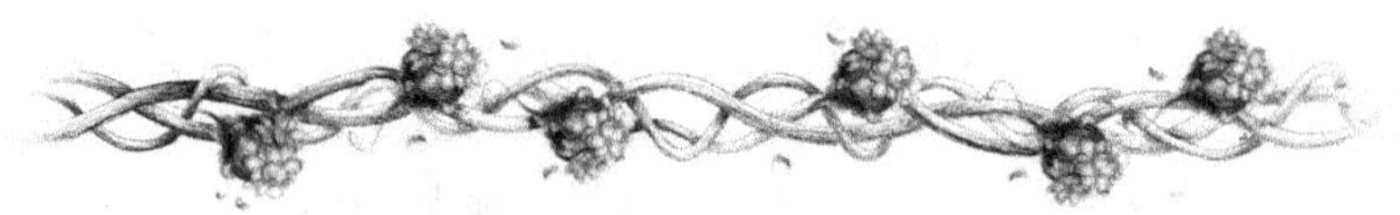

Joshua felt himself rousing. There was confusion at first. Disjointed images he couldn't understand rushed through his mind. Beaches, palm trees, colourful birds. It was like waking from a dream but the dream was drifting away quickly. *Was it a dream?* Joshua's senses slowly awoke. As they did, the images and thoughts faded. He struggled to hold onto them. He opened his eyes. At first everything was blurry but as he blinked, things became clearer. *Where am I?* He didn't recognise his surroundings. It was dark. Walls surrounded him. He blinked some more and the world came into focus. There was a figure lying next to him. He reached over to touch it. The figure stirred. Sarah turned her head and looked at him.

"Joshua? Is…is that you?" she said in a hazy state of confusion.

"W…where are we? I don't recognise this place."

Sarah sat up. She rubbed her eyes and scanned the room.

"I don't know. What just…happened? How did we get here?"

"I'm not sure," Joshua said, pushing himself into a seated position. "I don't know if…if I was dreaming or not. We were…" Joshua thought hard. "We were just…somewhere. I can't…"

"We were on a beach," Sarah said, concentrating hard. "It was…" She shook her head as if struggling to remember.

"What is this place?"

Joshua shook his head. They were sitting on a pile of sacks in a small, dimly lit room. A candle flickered beside them on a stone block. The walls were made from yellow stone. It was unlike anything Joshua had ever seen before. In the corner was a wooden door. Joshua stood up, helping Sarah to her feet.

Sarah scanned the dark room. Her eyes landed on a piece of parchment that lay next to the candle. Upon it was a red and green feather. Sarah reached for the feather and handed it to Joshua.

He turned to her suddenly as he remembered.

"Luana," he said tentatively. "Her name…was Luana."

Sarah put her hand to Joshua's face and caressed his cheek. "She cared for you…deeply." Sarah then took the parchment.

"There's something written on it," Joshua read:

*Hello Joshua. I know this must all be confusing to you. If you can remember her name, then all is not lost. I have left you something to help you to remember. I only pray that you do. If you want to live, you must come at once. He lives but He is weak. This makes Him desperate and even more dangerous than ever before. You are our only hope, Joshua. I pray your memory is still intact and that you can save us all.*

*- Yours hopefully, His Divine Majesty, King Ahmoses III*

The saga continues…

*If you want to find out what happens next with Joshua, check out the rest of the Portallas series with more instalments imminent:*

**Joshua and the Magical Forest**
*Portallas book 1*

**Joshua and the Magical Islands**
*Portallas book 2*

**Joshua and the Magical Temples**
*Portallas book 3*

**Joshua and the Magical Kingdoms**
*Portallas book 4*

# *Glossary*

## For full descriptions, visit
## **portallas.com**

**Alika**

Alika is the Protector of the island of Kihala, one of the
islands of Archipelago.

**Atoweena**

Atoweena is one of the larger island of Archipelago.
Located in the north, it is the island where Luana comes
from and where most of the inhabitants of Archipelago
live.

**Andrew**

Andrew was welcomed into the village of Morelle in
Forestium as an orphaned baby when he was just two
years old. Both his parents were killed in an earlier
skirmish during the tribal feuds that plagued the North
and West back then. Andrew grew up to be Joshua's best
friend.

## Dagger of Pa'hoa

The Dagger of Pa'hoa is a sacred object in Archipelago. Forged at the time Archipelago first came into existence, it has magical properties. It has been hidden for centuries, guarded by the Oracle. The Dagger is one of the few ways that Palm Crabs can be killed.

## Dauphins

Small fish that swarm in huge schools. Dauphin swarms can be manipulated into generating waves that can be surfed. This is one method used to travel between the islands of Archipelago.

## Epani

The only known Metamorph living in Archipelago.

## Goat

A mystical and reclusive magical being, the Goat is the embodiment of evil and malevolence. His origins are unclear. Half-man and half-goat, He spends much of his effort jealously guarding against anyone discovering the power behind various magical artefacts hidden throughout the worlds connected by the Portallas.

## Haluku

A small village on the north-eastern coast of the island of Atoweena. Haluku is where Luana and her sister were born.

## Hewa'luki

An enormous Palm Crab taller than a tree. Hewa'luki is
one of the Goat's dark creatures of the underworld that
was sent to wreak havoc and destruction throughout
Archipelago.

## Hulawei

One of the bigger villages on the island of Atoweena where
Luana currently lives.

## Imp

Imps are a diminutive race of people that have traditionally
lived in the Southern Tip, a peninsula in the far south of
Forestium. Galleon is an Imp.

## Joshua

Joshua was born in Morelle in Forestium's far west. He is
the firstborn child to Merinder and Sojath. Joshua grew
up an only child but survives a sister that died during
childbirth. Joshua's sister was not named and he was never
made aware of her brief existence.

## K'pia

A cone-shaped, barren rock just off the West coast of
Kuela's Nest Island, which marks the far western edge of
Archipelago. K'pia is the secret place of residence of the
Oracle (known in Archipelago as the Flame of Eternity).
The rock is exposed only during low tide.

## Kahu'niti

A reclusive shaman—the sole resident of the island of
Ulaia.

## Kalena

The younger sister of Luana, Kalena was Luana's only
other sibling. She was killed at a young age—believed to
be the work of Palm Crabs.

## Kakula grass

Long, thick stems of golden brown grass that grow on the northern slopes of Atoweena, in an area known as Panu'wahi. Clusters of sharp hook-like barbs grow around the stem long its length with flowers containing needles at the top. The bottom section of the stem is hollow.

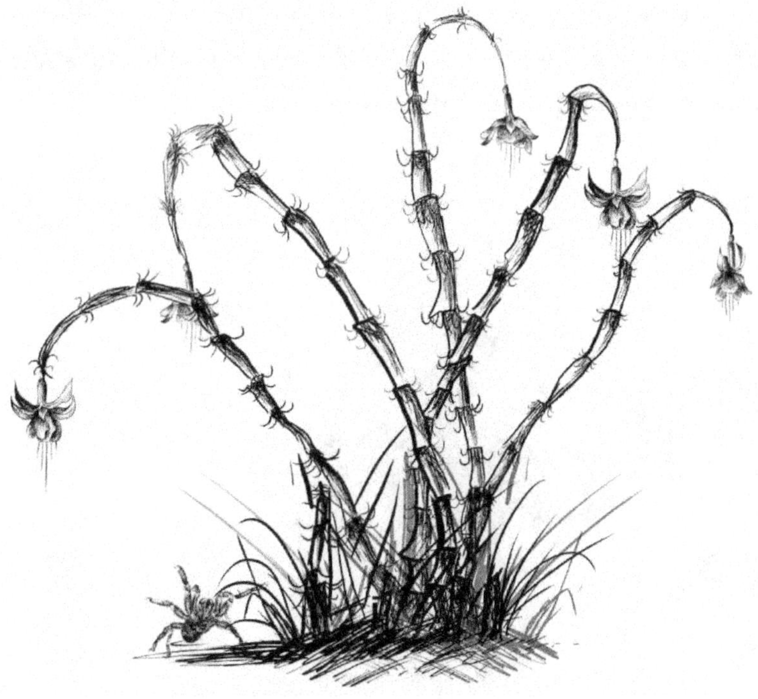

## Ke'ahi

The name given to an annual festival held on Atoweena to celebrate the summer solstice, where villagers of Piya'ata give thanks to the sun's life-giving properties.

## Kea'hee nuts

A red nut that grows is small bunches at the top of palm trees throughout Archipelago. With small flowers growing from them, they are comprised of husks, which can be opened to reveal numerous seedpods. The seedpods dissolve in water, releasing hundreds of tiny seeds that glisten when in contact with water. Pulling on the strand that grows from the bottom of a Kea'hee nut will cause it to ignite, making it useful for starting fires.

## Ki'koohoi

A huge, venomous spider found predominantly on the northern slopes of Atoweena, in an area known as Panu'wahi, avoided by villagers at all costs. This large spider's body is about as big as a fist and it produces luminous silk, which it weaves into balls. The spider lives mostly in caves and tunnels but comes out to hunt for prey in the Kakula grasses. A Ki'koohoi's bite is typically fatal.

## Kihala

One of the islands of Archipelago, located just south of Atoweena and east of Ulaia.

## Kuela

A beautiful, colourful bird with a long, yellow beak and long silvery blue tail feathers. It is prevalent throughout Archipelago. A huge colony exists on Kuela's Nest Island, which is where that island derives its name. Inhabitants of Archipelago can communicate with Kuelas, who can read their thoughts. The birds are often used to send messages between islands.

## Kuela's Nest Island

A small, rocky island connected to Atoweena via a sandbank that is visible during low tide. The island has little vegetation. It is the home to Archipelago's largest colony of Kuelas — hence the name.

## Lili'kio

An edible fruit that grows on Kuela's Nest Island. The green fruit tastes bitter until it has ripened, when it turns redder in colour.

## Lua'pele

The largest island of Archipelago—an uninhabited volcano.

## Luana

Luana is an inhabitant of Archipelago who lives on the island of Atoweena in the village of Hulawei. Luana never knew her parents, who both died when she was very young, but grew up in the care of her grandmother, Tu'hutu. She has a younger sister who was killed when she was young—presumed to have been taken by Palm Crabs during the night.

**Mano'ana**

A deadly eel that lives in the shallow waters of the west region of Archipelago. When active, Mano'ana can deliver a paralysing electric shock, which can cause a victim to drown. They have extremely sharp teeth.

**Metamorph**

An enigmatic race of beings with magical powers.
Metamorphs can change shape to become other people or
creatures. They also have healing powers. After hundreds
of years of persecution by the Goat, there are now but a
handful of Metamorphs spread out throughout the worlds
connected by the Portallas.

**Mirror of Prophecy**

Magical mirror—may be used to see briefly into the future.
Also provides a means for the Goat to see and reach into
Forestium.

**Opa'nu**

Edible fish, abundant throughout the waters of
Archipelago. The fish is silver with yellow stripes down its
length and a large dorsal fin sticking up from the top like a
fan.

## Oracle

An enigmatic being, the Oracle is known in Archipelago as the Flame of Eternity and takes the form of a small blue flame that levitates. Hidden within the hollow of a rock exposed only at low tide, known locally as K'pia, the Oracle's location is unknown to the inhabitants of Archipelago.

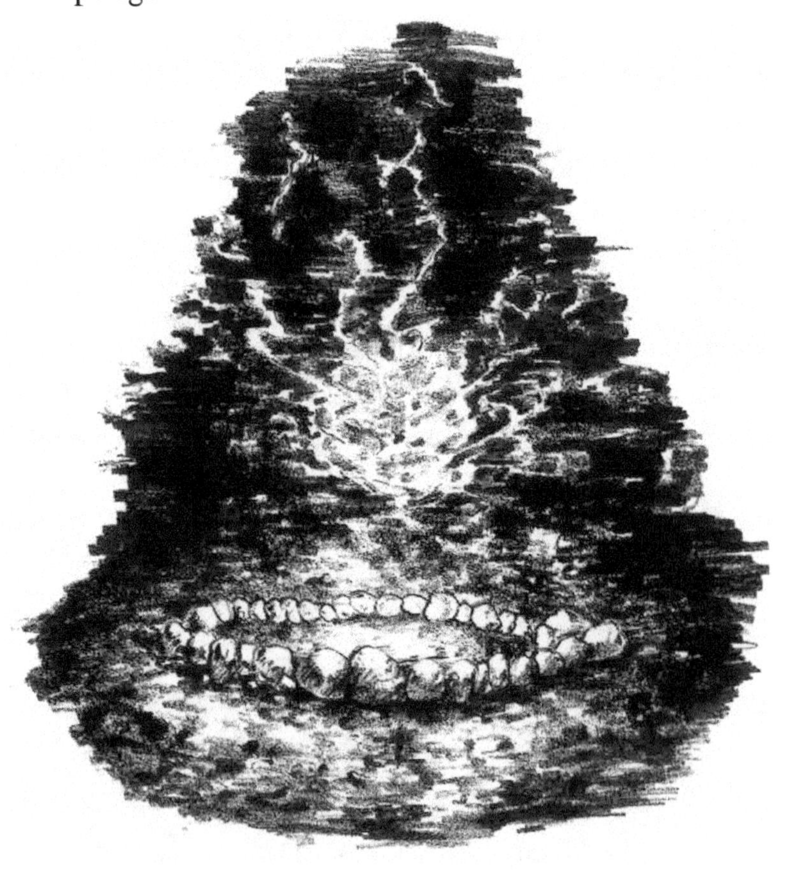

## Orb of Flight

Magical orb — calls forth the power of flight, which can transport you great distances in a short space of time.

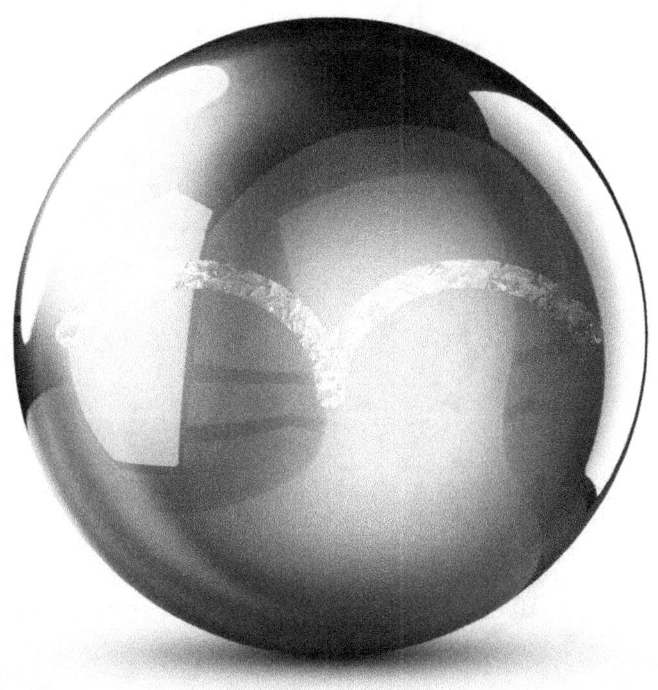

## Orb of Sacrifice

Magical orb—can only be activated when the one holding it dies.

## Orb of Sunshine

Magical orb—activated when in the presence of Palm Crabs, the orb emits intense rays that can stun or kill Palm Crabs when in close proximity to them.

## Paleki

Protector of Atoweena, the island where Luana lives.

## Palm Crab

Vicious dark creature of the underworld commanded by the Goat. Palm Crabs are huge crabs about the same size and mass as an adult human. They have a tough outer skeleton with huge pincers able to slice clean through bone. They are known to raid islands from time to time and kill. Palm Crab eyes emit light and their presence is typically preceded by the clicking sounds made by their pincers opening and shutting rapidly.

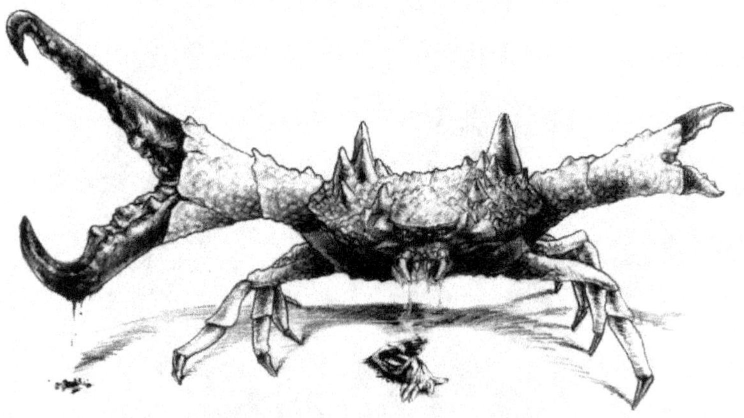

## Palm frond

The leaf from any one of a number of different types of a palm tree prevalent throughout Archipelago. Palm fronds have many practical uses.

## Panu'wahi

Name given to the northern slopes of Atoweena, which is avoided by locals due to the presence of deadly Ki'koohoi spiders that live throughout that region.

## Piya'ata

A village on the island of Atoweena, where Luana's grandmother, Tu'hutu' lives.

## Protector

Title given to the leader of a given island of Archipelago. Each inhabited island has a single Protector, who is responsible for all the island's villages and the wellbeing of its inhabitants. It is customary for the visitor of any island to first *check-in* with the local Protector.

## Sarah

Sarah is the only child of Serelle and Albert, now the Elder of Jemarrah in Forestium's far north. Although they have no other children of their own, Serelle and Albert took in an orphaned girl, Isabelle, when Sarah was very young and raised the adopted family member as their own. Sarah and Isabelle consider each other sisters and are very close. Sarah is a Fixer, someone who makes and mends things.

## Tu'hutu

A wise old woman that lives in the village of Piya'ata on the island of Atoweena. Tu'hutu is Luana's grandmother.

## Ulaia

A small island south of Atoweena and west of Kihala, where the reclusive hermit, Kahu'niti, lives. No other inhabitants occupy this island.

# About the author

Christopher Morgan is a New York Times & USA Today bestselling author, blogger, IT Manager, graphics artist, businessman, volunteer and family man currently living in Melbourne, Australia. He spends much of his spare time volunteering for his local community. He creates visual learning resources for primary school children, which he markets through his company Bounce Learning Kids. He is also involved in local civics and sits on various community and council committees. When he isn't writing, Christopher visits schools to deliver presentations on writing and being an author.

Christopher was born in the UK and grew up in England's South East. At age twenty, he moved to The Netherlands, where he married Sandy, his wife of 30 years. Christopher quickly learned Dutch and the couple spent 8 years living in the far South of that country before they moved to Florida in 1996. After spending 7 years in Florida, Christopher and Sandy sold their home and spent the next 2 years backpacking around the world. Christopher has visited over 40 countries to date.

Whilst circumnavigating the globe, Christopher wrote extensively, churning out travel journals. He and Sandy settled back in the UK at the end of their world tour, where their two children were both born. In 2009, the family moved to Melbourne, Australia, where they now live.

## Other books by Christopher D. Morgan

### Novels

*Joshua and the Magical Forest - Portallas book 1*

*Joshua and the Magical Islands - Portallas book 2*

*Joshua and the Magical Temples - Portallas book 3*

### Short stories

*Sarah's Farewell - A Portallas Short Story*

*Galleon's Prime - A Portallas Short Story*

*Andrew's Mission - A Portallas Short Story*

### Anthologies

*Ever in the After:*    A charity anthology in support of the 2017 Lift4Autism campaign.

*Dawn of Hope:*    A charity anthology in support of the Cajun Navy and their relief efforts for those affected by hurricanes Irma and Harvey.

www.ingramcontent.com/pod-product-compliance
Lightning Source LLC
Chambersburg PA
CBHW070439120726
47910CB00003B/855